Traci Douglass is a *USA TODAY* bestselling romance author for Mills & Boon, Entangled Publishing and Tule Publishing. She writes sometimes funny, usually awkward, always emotional stories, about strong, quirky, wounded characters overcoming past adversity to find their Happily Ever After. She believes Love is Love is Love, and is grateful for every thread in her intricate brocade of happiness—though she rarely remembers everything. Imperfect Characters = Perfect HEAs. Connect with her through her website: tracidouglass.net.

THE VET'S
UNEXPECTED
HERO

TRACI DOUGLASS

MILLS & BOON

First published in Great Britain 2021
by Mills & Boon, an imprint of HarperCollins*Publishers* Ltd,
1 London Bridge Street, London, SE1 9GF

www.harpercollins.co.uk

HarperCollins*Publishers*
1st Floor, Watermarque Building,
Ringsend Road, Dublin 4, Ireland

Large Print edition 2021

The Vet's Unexpected Hero © 2021 Traci Douglass

ISBN: 978-0-263-28813-1

11/21

To Charlotte, my editor extraordinaire,
who always has my back
and helps make my stories into
something worth reading.
Thank you!

CHAPTER ONE

DISASTERS USUALLY HAD most people running away from danger. EMT Jackson Durand wasn't most people.

His rig stopped outside the ambulance bay doors at Key West General ER and Jackson hopped out the back, followed closely by his EMT partner, Ned. Jackson's adopted brother, Dr. Luis Durand, met them at the entrance ready to take on the case.

"Forty-one-year-old firefighter with Key West FD," Jackson said as he and Ned lowered the gurney from the back of the rig down to the ground. "Riding his motorcycle and thrown from the bike, no loss of consciousness on scene. Obvious open left femur fracture."

The patient on the gurney moaned loudly and tried to get up, but Jackson held him in place with a hand on his chest as they wheeled him into the ER and down a brightly lit hall to an available trauma bay, picking up nurses and techs as they went.

"Sir," Luis said, stepping in beside Jackson. "Can you tell me your name?"

The patient bucked as they transferred him from the gurney to the hospital bed and one of the nurses lifted the sheet covering his lower body to look at the wound. "Reed," the man on the gurney said. "What's wrong with my leg? It hurts so bad."

"Your leg is broken, sir." Luis placed his stethoscope on the man's chest and listened before continuing. "Pretty badly, I'm afraid. But we're going to take good care of you." He nodded to Jackson then took over his brother's position at the patient's bedside. "Okay, we've got a good airway here. Good breath sounds bilaterally. Sir, can you open your eyes again for me? Looks like you're getting drowsy. Reed, can you wiggle your left toes for me?"

The patient screamed then, writhing on the bed. "Argh! It hurts…it hurts. I can't… I can't. My leg hurts so bad."

"Blood pressure?" Luis asked the nurse across the table.

"Seventy over forty, Doc."

Jackson hid his wince, barely. He felt for the guy. With an open compound fracture of the femur like that, it had to be sheer agony, but they couldn't risk giving him any pain meds for fear of his blood pressure dropping even lower, which would cause even more problems, including death if he stopped breathing.

"Right," Luis said. "Let's give him six units of blood, stat."

Jackson and Ned cleared the room to allow the staff more room to work. While Ned took the gurney back to the rig, Jackson headed down the hall to the supply room to stock up on supplies before his shift ended. Along the way, he greeted staff as they passed by. He knew just about everyone here and had a well-earned reputation as the go-to guy when it came to EMT services in the Keys. He liked being the man with the plan and the popularity that went with it. Mainly, though, he liked the control. Hopefully his rep would earn him a coveted promotion soon; he just needed a chance to prove himself.

He entered the supply room and began to fill his kit with fresh gauze packs, elastic bandages, syringes, gloves, and Steri-Strips. The neatly ordered shelves were a perfect reflection on his brother, Luis, who was the head of this department. Thoughtful, quiet, efficient. Everything in its place and a place for everything. All equal. Yep. That all fit Luis Durand to a tee. The complete opposite of Jackson, who thrived on chaos, quick decisions and excitement. Always better to keep moving, keep going, because those who fell behind got left behind.

He'd learned that lesson the hard way.

"Hey," a nurse said, coming around the corner of the aisle where he stood. She was dressed in pink scrubs with a jacket covered in cartoon babies. OB floor. Jackson's gaze flicked to her face then back to the supplies he was sorting through. She was cute, maybe late twenties, Asian. He didn't remember her name, but from the expectant smile on her face, she obviously remembered his. Probably because they'd gone out, had a good time, maybe more. He had a reputation outside the medical field, too.

"Hey," he said, not meeting her gaze. He wasn't embarrassed about his flings. He only slept with women who knew the score. No strings, no complications. If they'd been together, then she'd gone into it with her eyes open, too. He grabbed a handful of alcohol wipes and shoved them into the outer pocket of his pack, ignoring the hot prickle of her stare on the side of his face.

When he didn't say anything more, she stepped closer and smiled, shaking her head. "You don't remember me, do you?"

"Of course I do," he said, concentrating on the zipper of his pack and thinking maybe it was time to get out of the game. Not settle down, because he didn't do relationships—get in too deep and all you ended up with was heartbreak and disappointment—but his thirtieth birthday was coming up soon, and frankly he was getting too old for this crap. Maybe he'd get a dog or something to live on the houseboat with him. He hazarded a side glance at the name tag on her jacket. "How could I forget you, Susie?"

Her snort rang loud in the quiet supply room. "And that proves my point. I'm Amy. Borrowed this jacket earlier because I was cold." Heat crept up his neck as he straightened, hiding his wince. "But don't worry. I'm not offended," she said, jovially. "We hooked up at the St. Patrick's Day party at Durand's earlier this year. The night's pretty blurry for me, too, since we'd both had way too much to drink. It's all good."

Right.

His adoptive parents owned one of the most popular bars in the touristy section of Key West, Durand's Duck Bill Pub. He'd had a lot of good times at that bar—a lot of forgotten nights, too. He flashed her a slow smile, hoping his charm might get him out of another sticky situation. "Ah. Yes, right. I do remember you now, Amy. You won the green beer contest and hung a T-shirt from the rafters."

She shook her head and laughed. "I lost the whiskey duel and ended up having to kiss that gross leprechaun statue near the entrance. Nice try, though."

"Thanks." He winked and sidled past her. "Gotta go."

"Of course you do," she called as he walked out of the supply room fast. "Thanks for the memories."

"'Bye, Amy," he called back, glad to be out of the firing line. By the time he returned to the bustle of the ER, his brother was at the nurses' station barking orders into the phone to what Jackson assumed was the OR.

"Yes. Fireman thrown from his motorcycle with a known bad femur fracture. Suspected pelvic fracture. I'm also worried he may have an as-yet undiagnosed solid organ injury, perhaps liver or spleen, that's adding to the loss of blood. We'll need ortho to assist for the leg, but my primary concern right now is saving his life. Okay. Yes. I'll be up ASAP. Thank you."

"Another busy day in the neighborhood, huh?" Jackson moved in beside him at the counter and placed his refilled equipment pack at his feet. "You think he's going to make it?"

"I'm going to do everything I can to make sure he does," Luis said, heading toward the stairwell up to the third floor, only to be cut off by the man's family and fire crew. Jackson concentrated on filling out the requisition forms for his supplies while his brother did his best to put the new arrivals at ease. "Yes. Reed has got a bad leg fracture from the accident, and we're taking him to surgery now to repair it and also to make sure there's not more bleeding internally. If you have a seat in the waiting room, I'll be down as soon as I can with an update. I…"

His brother's voice trailed off and Jackson glanced up to see what had cause the rare occurrence. Luis was always well-spoken, always prepared, always on top of things. He had a mild case of Asperger's, so that kept him constantly thinking, constantly working through problems in his head that usually spilled out of his mouth as well. So, him going speechless was quite an event. But all Jackson saw were the same people as before. A middle-aged woman sobbing on the shoulder of a teenaged boy and girl, who he assumed were the patient's wife and kids. Behind them was Reed's fire crew in their uniforms, their fire truck parked outside the doors beside the ambulance, lights still blazing. Jackson recognized the firefighters, as they often went on the same runs as EMS, since many of them were trained as first responders as well. Bud Landry, John Cheeves and Stacy Williams. Luis definitely wasn't gay, so the guys were out as the source of Luis's sudden silence. Which left Stacy.

Blonde, twenty-seven or twenty-eight maybe. Pretty, in a natural, wholesome, beach bunny sort of way. Curvy and cute, but more than capable in the field and courageous as hell. Looks could definitely be deceiving in her case. Luis was staring at her like he'd seen a ghost.

Huh. Interesting. Maybe he'd been bitten by the love bug at last.

An overachiever in nearly every facet of his life except the personal, Luis pushed himself hard. Always working, always helping, always growing. He'd told Jackson once it was because his parents had died bringing him to the US from Cuba, sacrificed everything to give their son a better life. Luis felt obligated to live up to the legacy they'd given him, one of bravery and selflessness, even if doing so was to his own detriment. It was the one area he and Jackson had in common, but for very different reasons.

Luis's past was rooted in affirmation and acceptance. Jackson's in abandonment.

His mother had left him behind at four years old with no explanation and no word since.

He had no idea why she'd given him up, just that she had left him, and deep down he knew he probably deserved it.

The nearby elevators dinged and broke Jackson out of his thoughts. Seemed to break Luis out of whatever spell he'd fallen under, too. He excused himself and shoved into the stairwell like his butt was on fire. Jackson went back to finishing up his blasted paperwork, pushing the painful past away.

Of all the aspects of his job, the bureau-

cracy was his least favorite. He much pre-
ferred being out on runs, saving lives, helping
others, protecting those who needed it. In
fact, protection was his calling, his reason
for being. Plus, being an EMT meant he got
in, got out, got on with the next patient, never
getting too attached to any one person or
case. Attachment—that's where you really
got in trouble.

Because everyone left, sooner or later, once
they saw the real, unworthy you.

"Dude, I'm going to take off," Ned said,
clapping him on the shoulder as he walked
by, jarring Jackson out of his thoughts. "You
need anything from the rig before I go?"

"Nah, man. Thanks." Jackson planned
to use the staff locker room downstairs to
shower and change after his shift before
heading to the latest meeting of the local
emergency response team in the hospital conference room. He was incident commander
for this one, and if things went well, it could
lead to him landing the recently vacated regional director spot for the local ambulance
authority.

"Oh, wait," Jackson said, initialing and signing on the dotted lines. "You can take this full pack back with you if want."

"Will do. I'm going to run down to the cafeteria and get a soda real quick first, then I'll be back to get it. Sure you don't want anything?" Ned asked as he walked over to the elevators.

"No. Thanks, man. Have a good rest of your shift." Jackson smiled over at his partner. If he got in and out of the showers fast enough, he'd grab a bite himself before the meeting. Coming off a twelve-hour rotation, he needed time to wind down, though, before thinking about a meal. "Take your time."

Jackson flipped to yet another sheet on his clipboard and started on the next form, only half listening to the drone of the TV in the waiting room behind him.

"Tropical Storm Mathilda is expected to strengthen into a major hurricane by the time it reaches the Gulf early next week. As of right now, projections are still vague as to exactly where the eyewall will make landfall, but we do expect it to at least brush the Keys on its way toward mainland USA."

Jackson sighed. Another early August day in southern Florida. They'd been having meetings off and on since the start of the hurricane season in May. Each week a few new faces appeared in the conference room, and the team was rounded out as conditions changed. The incident commander's job was to coordinate all the different team members into a cohesive whole and direct their resources to the areas that needed them most during the crisis. Considering he'd worked as an EMT in Key West since leaving the coast guard four years ago, and had pretty much seen and heard it all, it was a task he was well prepared for. Plus, he loved what he did. But he also had more to contribute, and being named regional director would give him that opportunity.

Jackson dotted the last i and crossed the last t on his paperwork, then handed it back to the nurse behind the desk, just as a female voice behind him asked, "Excuse me. Can you tell me where the conference room is, please? I'm here for the ERT meeting."

He turned to see a petite, dark-haired woman with a huge, panting golden retriever at her side. The dog was almost as big as she was, with a goofy doggo grin on its face, tongue lolling, and a red therapy vest on its back. Jackson couldn't resist crouching to scratch the pup behind the ears. "Who's a good boy, huh?"

"His name is Sam, and he's working," the woman said, her tone edged with annoyance this time. "Directions, please? I don't want to be late."

Jackson glanced back up into her anxious dark eyes. He straightened and gave her a polite smile. "Sorry. I should've asked to pet him first. Come on. I'll show you the way." He stowed the pack for Ned with the nurse behind the desk then gestured for the woman to follow him. "You're way too early, though. Meeting doesn't start until three. It's only two now."

"I know." She moved around him, and the

dog trotted obediently at her side. "I'd rather be early. I always like to be prepared."

They walked out of the ER and into a quiet corridor leading to the administrative wing. He gave her a side glance, their shoes squeaking on the shiny linoleum and the dog's leash jangling in time to the clatter of its nails on the floor. Trying to ease the awkward with humor, he joked, "Isn't that the Boy Scout motto? Always be prepared."

"Could be. I really wouldn't know." She stared straight ahead, her steps evenly measured to avoid all the cracks between tiles. Hmm. Her cheeks were pink, too, and he couldn't tell if it was because it was hot outside—almost ninety today—or if she was still mad he'd petted her dog. Either way, it was clear she wanted nothing to do with him.

At the end of the hall, they reached a doorway marked with a gold plaque that read Conference Room A. She gave a curt nod and finally faced him, though she kept her gaze fixed on the dog. "Thank you."

"Uh, sure." He slowly backed away, more intrigued than he cared to admit. People liked him. Women liked him a lot. Except for this one. She posed a puzzling challenge, and he did love a challenge. The list of new team members ran through his head as he tried to pinpoint her identity. "I'll see you later, then."

Confusion flickered across her pretty features, and she frowned. "Why?"

"I'll be in the ERT meeting, too. Jackson Durand, by the way. That's my name."

He waited for her to tell him hers, but she didn't. Just led her big old dog into the conference room, then closed the door behind her.

Lucy Miller took a seat on the far side of the large, empty table in the conference room and released her pent-up breath. Eyes closed, she repeated her mantra, the words her therapist had given her a few months earlier to lower her anxiety.

You can do this. You're in control.

Near her feet, Sam curled into a big ball and went to sleep, sighing deeply. She was exactly fifty-nine minutes early, and that was fine by her. Of course, a nice round number would've been better. Two hours. That had been her goal, but then she'd gotten waylaid by people in the ER and had to ask for directions and...ugh.

Her shoulders slumped, and her tote bag slipped down her arm into her lap.

No. It was fine. Everything was fine. She fought back against the voice in her head that whispered that without her routines, without her counting and control, everything would slip into chaos. That she was broken. That she wasn't capable of handling life or even the simplest tasks by herself. Those were lies. Fed to her by the people closest to her, the ones she should've been able to trust.

Her family and her fiancé. Well, ex-fiancé now.

Stupid Robert.

But she was capable. She was strong. She was self-reliant. That's what her therapist had said, and that's what she tried to believe.

Even if some days were harder than others.

Of course, being in an unfamiliar place made her issues worse, as did stressful situations and strange people. Normally, she tried to avoid all of it by staying safe and happy in her private animal sanctuary on Big Pine Key. Her medication helped, too, especially on days like today, when she forced herself to go out and meet her obligations, like volunteering with her therapy animals in the children's ward of Key West General. Today it was with Sam, but she also had a cockatoo named Bubba she brought along too sometimes. Bubba was molting at the moment, however, so not looking his best.

The blast of cold air from the vent above her head felt good on her heated cheeks, and she put her head back to enjoy it a bit. Getting here early, finding the seat she wanted—not too close to anyone else, and with a clear path to the exit—helped. As did the silence, the stillness. It was like having her own little nook where no one would bother her. Nice. She tipped her head forward again and looked down the table toward the front of the room. There was a window. And a plant. A whiteboard and a podium for the speakers.

She wouldn't be speaking, thank goodness. Honestly, she was only here as a favor to a friend at the local animal shelter. Her friend had said that during evacuations due to hurricanes, the local animal shelters often became overrun with pets left behind, and they needed her sanctuary to take in additional animals after the latest storm, Mathilda, blew through. They'd asked her about search and rescue, too, but she didn't have any trained dogs at the moment, only Sam. Her good buddy. The bestest boy.

Jackson Durand had been right about that, at least.

His handsome face flashed into her mind again. Strong, compelling, his smile warm and inviting.

Stay away, the alarm bells blared in her head.

No. Lucy wasn't looking for love or any other kind of relationship, not after Robert and his betrayal. Since breaking off her toxic engagement, she'd sworn off men—sworn off new connections of any kind, really—after escaping the controlling, manipulative clutches of those she'd left behind in Charleston.

Lucy took a deep breath to ease the coiling anxiety inside her those memories always brought, ready to strike at any moment. She'd trusted them to have her best interests at heart, only to find they wanted to keep her basically locked inside a cage, locked inside her disabilities, until she doubted everything, including her own ability to survive. Her chest squeezed with hurt, and her breath caught.

Focus on the numbers. The numbers make you feel better.

There'd been forty-seven steps from the time they'd left the ER to this conference room. She'd not stepped on one crack. That was good. A new record. Her OCD had her counting like that a lot. How many steps from one place to another, how many hairbrush strokes to untangle her hair each morning, how many keystrokes to fill up one new patient intake form for her animal clinic.

She'd gotten her doctorate in veterinary medicine just to prove her family and Robert wrong.

Well, that and she loved animals. They

never lied. Never betrayed you. You could trust animals.

A few more people arrived, none of whom were Stacy Williams, the only other person she knew on the team. Lucy sat forward to fiddle in her tote bag, setting out her legal pad and pens just so. Then, restless and overstimulated, she pulled out a mirror to check her face. Still there. Still the same. Still "just so."

Honestly, living a life of "just so" was exhausting.

If she could've stopped, she would have, but the idea of not counting, not arranging, not giving in to her tics only made her anxiety worse, so...

No. It had been a hard-fought battle the last two years, first leaving Charleston, then moving to Key West, but she'd finally come to accept who she was, painful as it had been. She didn't need other people. She didn't need romance. She didn't need affection. All she needed was peace and quiet and space to live the life that was best for her. Alone. Because alone didn't hurt you or smother you or make you feel broken.

Being on her compound, with her animals, gave her a level of peace she'd never known before. And if she still got lonely some nights, well, that was a small price to pay for peace of mind.

Up until today, she'd hoped that peace of mind would stay forever, but then she'd heard the weather reports and— *Oh, boy.*

Any thought of the approaching tropical storm had those knots of tension inside her tightening. Which was silly. Storms and hurricanes were a part of life in this area of the world. She'd been warned about that when she'd bought her property. The previous owners had taken good precautions to prevent property damage as well, including storm shutters and structural reinforcements. But still…

Her throat constricted, and her pulse tripped.

If she lost her sanctuary, she wasn't sure what she'd do. She had to make sure it was safe, no matter what. So, she planned to stay there and ride out the storm. Didn't matter what the experts recommended or what Stacy thought she should do. She'd grown up in

Charleston and they'd had plenty of hurricanes, even if her family's home there had been far from the coast. She could handle it. She wasn't going to budge. She'd protect the house, board up the windows, secure the pens, batten down the hatches. She'd moved down here to be brave, and that's what she was going to do.

You can do this. You're in control.

"There you are. Sorry I'm late," Stacy said, sitting down next to her at the table. "I saw you in the ER before with Jackson, then you disappeared on me. I thought maybe he'd worked his magic on you and stolen your heart. He's got a reputation as a player, you know?"

Lucy frowned, remembering the man who'd walked her here. He was gorgeous, she supposed, if you went for that whole tall and muscled type, with his smooth mocha skin and soulful green-gold eyes. Not that she'd noticed. Nope. The player part she could totally see, too. He'd been far too charming for his own good.

Stacy laughed as Sam turned excited circles in front of her. Everyone loved her dog, and the feeling was mutual. He was friendly and outgoing and gregarious. Basically, everything his owner wasn't. Lucy tugged once gently on the dog's leash to get him to sit, an odd ache in the pit of her stomach.

"How many people will be in this meeting?" Lucy asked as more and more arrivals filled the room. She resisted the urge to fiddle with her pens once again, and her lungs ached slightly as her anxiety spiked once more. Having Stacy there helped. Her best friend was one of the kindest, most generous, most loyal people Lucy knew. She was beautiful, inside and out, and her son, Miguel was an angel, too. They visited her at the sanctuary on the weekends sometimes. Miguel was mildly autistic, and being with the animals helped him developmentally. In fact, Lucy was helping Stacy acquire a therapy dog for him from a trainer in Miami.

"Twenty, maybe thirty people," Stacy said, tucking a piece of sun-streaked blond hair that had come loose from her ponytail behind her ear. "I know busy places can be hard for you sometimes. They're hard for Miguel as well." She pulled out her phone and scowled down at the screen. "Sorry. They brought in one of the guys from my crew earlier to the ER."

"Oh gosh." Lucy's anxiety was tempered with concern. That explained the slight gray tinge to her friend's tanned complexion. "Is it serious?"

"Badly fractured leg, possibly some internal bleeding as well. He's in surgery now."

"What happened? Was it a fire?"

"No. This was Reed's day off. He was riding his motorcycle and went off the road." Stacy set her phone on the table, screen down. "They'll know more once he wakes up. If he wakes up."

"I'm so sorry."

Lucy had never been on a motorcycle. She never took unnecessary risks. They scared her too badly.

"Thanks." Stacy nodded, frowning. "His family is here now, waiting. Funny, isn't it? How one moment can change everything."

For some odd reason, she got the feeling

her friend was talking about more than just a motorcycle accident. Lucy placed her hand on Stacy's atop the table. "Everything okay?"

"Yes. No. I don't know. Something else happened in the ER. I saw someone I didn't think I'd ever see again and now—"

"Hello, hello," a now-familiar voice said from the front of the room.

Lucy looked up to find Jackson Durand, freshly showered and changed, and her pulse tripped despite her wishes. She swallowed hard and grabbed the pen closest to her, tapping it on the table with relief.

Hurricane Mathilda might be on the way, but something told her this man was far more dangerous.

CHAPTER TWO

"Right, so, as your incident commander, I'm officially calling this meeting of the Lower Keys Community Emergency Response Team for Tropical Storm Mathilda to order," Jackson said from behind the podium. "Let's start with Assistant Fire Chief Stacy Williams with an update on the training program for posthurricane cleanup volunteers in the area."

As Stacy moved to take over, Jackson refocused his attention on the woman he'd escorted here earlier. She was sitting in her seat, still tapping that pen, her big dog at her feet like a shield. She'd pushed her chair back slightly now, he noticed, and turned it to face the front of the room, giving him a view of her feet bouncing on the floor like she was excited or nervous. And sure, the impending storm got everyone's adrenaline pumping, but this situation was nothing out of the ordinary for this part of the world.

Jackson frowned. He'd been through countless storms growing up. It was part of being a Conch—the nickname people affectionately gave native Key Westerners. Watching his intriguing new stranger, though, had him thinking her fidgeting was something more. Given the way she always seemed to be fiddling with her pens or papers or whatever, he wondered if she had some kind of disorder—anxiety, OCD maybe, or both...

Luis sneaked in silently through the door then leaned against the wall beside Jackson. It wasn't like his brother to be late, but with the surgery on that motorcycle accident patient, it wasn't unexpected. He gave his brother a side glance, noticing again how he seemed transfixed by Stacy at the front of the room.

Concerned, Jackson whispered, "Everything okay?"

"What?" Luis started, then blinked several times, as if just then remembering where he was. He glanced over at Jackson, scowling before his usual professional mask slid back into place. "Fine. Just tired. And preoccupied by my case. What did I miss?"

"Nothing much. We just started," Jackson said, still not convinced there wasn't more going on.

Exhaustion went with being in the medical profession. In fact, Jackson was pretty sure it was at the top of the job description for both of them. Paramedics and doctors and nurses, especially those on the front lines in the emergency department, worked crazy shifts. And both Durand brothers pushed themselves to the limits every day. Jackson striving to prove himself worthy and Luis because he was basically superhuman. Okay, maybe that was exaggerating, but it certainly felt that way to Jackson sometimes. Two years older, Luis had been pushing himself for as long as Jackson had known him. Growing up together in their adopted household, having Luis to look up to was both a blessing and a curse. His older brother's lofty goals and selfless work gave Jackson an ever-shifting finish line to try to reach that kept him working harder, longer, faster, better—even if he'd never get to Luis's pinnacle. It was fine. Jackson strove to meet his own high standards and surpass the expectations of those around him, because maybe then he wouldn't get left behind.

And speaking of left behind...

"Who's the new person over there?" Jackson asked, hiking his chin toward the woman who'd been invading his thoughts for the past hour or so. "Do you know her?"

Before Luis could answer, Stacy said from the podium, "And I'd like to welcome my friend veterinarian Lucy Miller here today. She runs an animal sanctuary on Big Pine Key and will be assisting the local animal shelter in housing displaced animals after the storm. Everyone, say hello to Lucy."

Jackson watched as Lucy visibly withdrew into herself under the scrutiny, and he cringed inwardly for her. Stacy meant well, he was sure, but man, all that attention had to be excruciating for such an obvious introvert.

"You didn't tell me she would be here," Luis whispered.

Jackson was confused by the vehemence in his brother's voice. "Who? Stacy?"

He hadn't mentioned it because he didn't think it mattered. As far as he knew, Luis didn't know Stacy, but it was clear from his brother's expression he'd been wrong. Normally, he'd prod for more information about that, since any crack in his brother's perfect armor was a rare and powerful thing, but before he could do so, Stacy wrapped up her presentation.

"And with that, I'll turn things back over to IC Jackson Durand, who will update us on the EMS response plans for Hurricane Mathilda," she said.

Right. Time to get back to work.

Jackson jogged back up to the podium. "Thanks, Stacy. As you all know, EMTs are likely to be the first on the scene of a disaster. As per our usual protocol, we take charge of the incident and remain so until it's resolved or others who have legal authority assume responsibility. This won't change with Hurricane Mathilda. When EMTs arrive at the scene of an emergency related to this storm, we'll implement the incident command system listed in the binders before you.

As incident commander, I've established our command post here at Key West General and will receive updates from all quadrants of our combined efforts and will then provide an assessment of the overall situation to local officials and media, identify response resources required and direct the on-scene response from here at our central ICP."

He'd served as a member of these teams for years now and knew the speech backward and forward, though this was the first time he was giving it as IC. It felt both surreal and super special. His chest swelled with pride and a pinch of hurt. Briefly, he wondered what his birth mom might think of him now, being in charge of such an important event. But then he shoved that thought aside quickly. She wouldn't know or care about his accomplishments, because she'd refused to have any contact with him for the last twenty-five-plus years. He finished his report, then turned the podium over to the chief of police to discuss law enforcement's preparations for the storm.

Good thing, too, since his attention kept

returning to Lucy Miller. The name suited her. Short, sweet and no-nonsense. She stared back at him, her dark eyes wide, her long hair tied back into a neat ponytail at the base of her neck with a light green scrunchie the exact same color as the top she was wearing. Her cheeks were flushed, and dark brows knit. She crossed her arms, fingers tapping on her skin, three times. Stop. Three more times.

Yep. Definitely something going on there.

"That's right isn't it, IC?" the police chief asked, and Jackson found himself at a loss.

Crap. He cleared his throat and stared down at the notes in front of him, trying to get his head back in the game. This wasn't like him. He was Mr. Efficiency. Mr. Two Steps Ahead of Everyone Else, because he had to be. Mr. Get the Job Done. This was ridiculous. He had important things to do here. Way more important than watching some woman he'd just met, no matter how attractive.

"Weather," Luis whispered helpfully from where he'd taken a seat at the table.

"Right. Current reports have Mathilda veering west of the Keys with only the possibility of some minor outer band involvement as she passes. Therefore, our current readiness level is staying at three. If the path of the storm changes however, we will update the status appropriately. Please keep your phones on and be ready to respond to any alerts. Also, remember that if the readiness level reaches one, all team members are required to shelter in place within the city limits of Key West for the duration, so prepare accordingly for that as well. Might not come to that, God willing, but better safe than sorry."

Jackson shuffled his notes, his gaze flicking back to Lucy again. She was chatting quietly with Stacy now, who'd taken a seat beside her at the table again, and Lucy smiled at something Stacy said. And man, what a smile that was. Like a sunbeam breaking through the clouds above. A good smile.

A beautiful smile.

His gut clenched, and he looked away fast. Nope. He frowned then shifted his attention to the cop's presentation. Jackson had no time for this. He was busy building his career. If he did well as IC, it could land him the regional director position, which would lead to more money, more prestige, better benefits and a bigger home, instead of the tiny houseboat he currently resided in. Not that his life was bad. It was fine. Good. But he'd never been one to settle for good, and Jackson wasn't about to start now, because the idea of staying put and committing to one person, heart and soul, scared the bejesus out of him. Besides, he'd been burning the candle at both ends for years for this opportunity. He was not about to blow it now over a woman.

He checked his watch. After the current speaker, there were closing remarks, then the meeting would be over and he could get back to work, back to life, back to not thinking about Lucy Miller with her dark eyes and sweet smile and distracting, irritating, intriguing issues.

Lucy sat through the meeting, taking notes as appropriate and doing her best not to think about the man watching her across the table like she was his new favorite science experiment. Dammit. She still couldn't believe

Stacy had introduced her to the whole group like that without warning. She avoided the spotlight like most people avoided wasps' nests.

At least the meeting was over now, and people were clearing out. Sam whined from near her ankle, his tail thumping against her chair a mile a minute as passersby stopped to give him a pat on the head. Extrovert that he was, Sam loved it. And it helped divert attention from Lucy, so win-win.

Or most attention, she should say, as the man she'd done her best to ignore for the last hour slid into the seat beside her that Stacy had recently vacated.

"Nice to meet you, Lucy Miller," Jackson said, watching her with his mesmerizing gold-green gaze.

Heat prickled her cheeks, and she avoided looking at him. The fact he could sit there all composed and grinning after not telling her up front he was head of this whole thing made her want to kick him in the shin. Unfortunately, Sam was all over the guy, blocking her target.

Instead, she tried to kill him with kindness, keeping her voice polite and pleasant. "Did you need something?"

He didn't answer right away, and she finally gave in and looked at him. Big mistake. The glimmer of interest in his eyes, coupled with a hint of irritation, rattled her completely. Fresh anxiety bubbled inside her like lava, and to ease it, she picked up her purple pen and squeezed it tight.

Except disturbing the specific order she'd laid her items out in on the table always triggered her compulsions and...whoops. Here it came. Unable to stop herself, she glanced at the rest of her pens still lined up in a neat little row. Red, blue, black, green. Red goes first. Always, always, always. She used red the most. It made sense. If she used it the most, then it had to come first. Somewhere in her mind, she knew the voice in her head telling her this had nothing to do with reality and everything to do with her OCD, but she couldn't stop.

You can do this. You're in control.

Yes. She was in control of her condition.

Not the other way around. If she wanted to move the stupid red pen, then she could. She had the power to move it...

"You all right, Lucy?" Jackson asked, his eyes narrowing. "You seem flustered."

She looked over at him, helplessness choking her throat. Because once her anxiety set in, her sole focus was on her pens. She'd taken her meds before coming here today, but then getting lost in the ER and the stress of the meeting had made her symptoms worse. She should've doubled up on her dose like her therapist had said. Next time she would.

Stupid Lucy. Poor, weak, broken Lucy.

"Hey..." Jackson leaned forward in his seat, uncrossing his long legs to rest his forearms on his knees. Sam took that as an invitation and immediately launched himself into the guy's lap, all sixty pounds of him. Soon, his face was covered with wet doggy kisses as he tried to see past the mass of fur in front of him.

"Oh God." The shock of it jarred Lucy out of her anxiety spiral at last, and she scrambled to get her errant pet off his lap. "I'm so sorry. He's usually much better behaved than this."

Jackson chuckled and shrugged, wiping the sleeve of his blue T-shirt over his face. "It's fine. I tend to have that effect on people, though usually it's women."

Lucy snorted, more as a stress reliever than anything. "Overconfident much?"

"Always," he countered, grinning. Then he leaned an elbow on the table, bumping her pens and scattering them.

He didn't do it on purpose. Lucy knew that, but it was still a battle for her not to freak out. Her first instinct was to straighten them out again, reorder them. Except she couldn't do so without touching him, because his elbow was right there. She took a deep breath.

"Okay?" he asked.

"Sure," she said, with far more enthusiasm than required.

Perfect.

If he noticed, at least he didn't say anything, thank goodness.

"I wanted to stop by and introduce myself properly, since we didn't get a chance to before the meeting." He held out his hand over her messy pens. "Jackson. Jackson Durand."

I don't care, I don't care, I don't care. My pens are out of order...

"Nice to meet you," she said.

Then it became too much and Lucy swiped her hand as quickly as possible over the pens, sorting them, straightening them, grazing his elbow in the process. She ignored his hand completely.

Jackson blinked then sat back, watching her closely. "So, you're a vet?"

"That's right." Lucy concentrated on the pens and not him, afraid of what she'd see in his eyes. "Why?"

"No reason." He shrugged. "I could've handed those to you."

"Handed me what?" Her mind whirled with competing demands. First, her OCD wanted her to line up those damned pens again. Second, her reasonable side told her to let it go and talk to the handsome man beside her. Unfortunately, her OCD won, so she placed her pens back on the table again, lining them each up a second time with the edge. Red, blue, black, green, purple. Evenly spaced. Just so.

She kept her eyes glued to her task, particularly the red pen screaming at her to get the heck out of there and get back to her sanctuary. This whole meeting had messed with her schedule, big-time. Lucy lived by her schedule. Each day, she wrote out a list and crossed every item off before she was done. Today had included cleaning out Bubba's cage, then there was checking on Mitzi's egg mound and, as always, feeding and walking Sam. Now she'd have to add making sure she had enough supplies to last for a few days in case the storm was worse than predicted, because she sure as heck wasn't leaving her compound, rules or not and...

Speaking of Sam... She looked up at Jackson. "He's trained to be a therapy dog. He knows better than to jump up on people like that."

"Really. It's okay. I'm used to it. Like I said, some people find me irresistible." Jackson gave her a charmingly crooked, wry smile she felt all the way to her toes.

Oh boy. Not good. Not good at all.

Lucy needed something, anything, to distract herself from her unwanted awareness of this man. "Fine. Whatever. Good for you if people find you irresistible. I don't. I mean, there's nothing wrong with you, but—"

He crossed his arms, his smile widening as she babbled away like an idiot.

Her cheeks felt hotter than Hades now, and the more he teased her, the more frazzled she got. "What I'm trying to say is you are who you are, and I am who I am, and people don't change who they are."

God, where had *that* come from?

Jackson studied her, his expression serious. "Okay. But what if they're a jerk?"

"Oh, well…" Flustered, Lucy forgot to be nervous and just laughed, easing some of her inner tension. She shrugged and stared down at her toes. "Point taken."

"Well, it was nice to meet you, Lucy Miller," he said, clasping his hands atop the table. Those were nice hands. Long, tapered fingers, well-kept nails. Strong hands. Capable hands. He was a paramedic, after all. He saved people. A small spark of warmth burst inside her. He'd certainly saved her just now, from dying from terminal embarrassment. "I wish I'd known earlier you were going to be here. I'd have brought a copy of the required binder with the emergency response team plan for you. I don't have a spare with me now, but if you give me your address, I'm happy to run one by your place on Big Pine Key tomorrow. It's my day off."

"Oh...uh..." Sitting beside him in the conference room was disturbing enough to her equilibrium. The thought of him at her compound had her quaking in her tennis shoes. "That's okay. Give it to Stacy and she can bring it to me. Or I can swing by the hospital and pick it up." She pulled a clean sheet of paper from her legal pad and picked up her red pen. "Just tell me what time would be best."

Jackson frowned. "It's really no problem, and it would be more convenient for me to drop it off. I'll be in your area, anyway. Unless there's some reason you don't want me there?"

An awkward silence fell between them as they studied each other.

She couldn't help wondering what it might feel like to slide her fingers through his short black hair, learning its texture and temperament. The fluorescent overhead lights gleamed off his high cheekbones and there was a hint of dark stubble on his firm jaw. His lips were full and firm, with a slight tip to the outer corners that gave him a perpetual smirk, like everything amused him. Maybe it did.

"Don't worry, I won't overstay my welcome. Promise. I'll google your address," he said at last. Jackson stood and picked up his papers but didn't hold out his hand this time. The smile was there again, though, still charming, too. "See you tomorrow, Lucy Miller."

Her heart stumbled a bit before racing forward.

"Uh, yeah." Lucy pushed to her feet as well, staring at his retreating back. Wide shoulders, narrow waist, trim hips. She forced her attention back to gathering her own supplies as Sam whined at her feet, panting up at her with his lopsided doggy grin as if telling her to get a move on already. "All right, mister. We're going."

CHAPTER THREE

THE NEXT AFTERNOON, Lucy stood in the small clinic building on her compound in Big Key Pine, tending to Bubba the cockatoo. He was approximately fifteen years old and nearly bald at the moment, except for the still magnificent crown atop his head. His previous owner had died shortly after Lucy had opened her sanctuary, and her good friend and fellow vet on the island, Dr. Dave, had felt she and Bubba might be a good fit.

Said owner had also loved music, apparently, since Bubba had a tendency to quote lyrics at the most inappropriate times. "Come on, Bubba. Take your medicine. There you go. There's a pretty boy, yes. Eat that orange wedge. Yes. Good birdie."

Sam sat near her feet, whining, and Lucy rolled her eyes. "You don't get oranges. And you just had a treat, anyway."

Bubba eyed her warily but continued munching on the orange wedge clutched in his foot with the pill tucked safely inside, bobbing his head as the door to her clinic banged opened and Jackson backed in.

Usually her work focused her and cleared her head, keeping her anxiety at bay like nothing else. But one look at Jackson and her nerves went haywire again. Bubba seemed to sense her disquiet, because he began dancing back and forth on his perch, what was left of the orange slice stuck to the side of his beak, crooning, "Swee-ee-ee-t emo-o-o-o-tion..."

"It's okay," she said to soothe the bird as much as herself as her trusty canine companion trotted across the room to greet the new arrivals enthusiastically. "It's going to be okay."

She did not have emotions for Jackson Durand, sweet or otherwise, because she never let anyone that close. Not anymore. Lucy raised her chin and snapped her fingers, bringing Sam back to her side. "You're late."

"Sorry. I know." He turned then, the binder he'd promised tucked under one arm and a squirming, mewling bundle wrapped in a beach towel filling his hands. "But I ran into a bit of a problem."

Lucy frowned. "What's going on? What is that?"

He rushed over and set the bundle carefully on her exam table. "I was on my way back here from Miami and found this little guy on the side of the highway."

Her veterinary training took over, immediately drowning out everything else, including her thundering pulse from Jackson's closeness. "Right." She gestured for him to stay put, then pulled on a pair of gloves. "Any idea what happened?"

"Not sure. Like I said, I was coming back from the mainland and spotted something squirming out of the corner of my eye near the median. When I realized what it was, I had to stop. I was on my way here, so figured you might be able to help."

"I'm glad you did." Carefully, she unwrapped the towel from around her new arrival and took stock of the situation. Small Bengal kitten. Male. Eyes barely open. Lethargic. Underweight. Five, maybe six weeks old. Trembling. Back left leg severed below the knee. Wound clotting and not actively bleeding.

"He must've got caught in traffic." Or been thrown out by careless owners. Biting the inside of her cheek, Lucy forced her anger down. "Stand here with him while I get my supplies, please."

"Sure thing," Jackson said, stroking the kitten's matted fur with a finger as he crooned softly to him.

Lucy grabbed a saline IV bag and popped it into the microwave nearby she'd installed for this purpose. While the saline solution heated, she pulled out a warming blanket and plugged it in before sliding it under, then wrapping it around, the tiny feline. Finally, she snatched an otoscope from the front pocket of her denim overalls and leaned over to look in the kitten's ears. Next she checked its mouth. The gums were pale, but its teeth looked fine. Checked its temperature, too. Low, but not nearly as down as she'd hoped.

The way some people treated animals was

reprehensible. By the look of that leg, the poor thing had probably been crushed by a tire, or perhaps caught in a trap. Wouldn't be the first time she'd seen that around here. Unfortunately, it was an all-too-common occurrence in these parts, with alligators everywhere. In fact, the sanctuary's longest resident had been the victim of the same kind of trap. It was inhumane.

Lucy put the used thermometer in the sink for sterilizing, then rolled her tense shoulders to relax them. Mistreatment of any kind made her furious.

Maybe that was why she'd built such a strong barrier around her heart. Robert might not have hurt her physically, but he'd abused her heart and her trust, and for that, she couldn't forgive him. It was because of him she wouldn't let anyone else near again. Opening up her emotions meant letting the good in with the bad, so it was better just to not care at all. At least where humans were concerned. With animals, it was a whole different ball game.

She shoved the buds of her stethoscope in

her ears and listened to the kitten's heart, lungs and abdomen. Nothing worrisome. BP was good, too. The little guy lifted his head and whimpered when Lucy tried to better examine the leg.

"I know, sweetie. It hurts, huh? I'll get you something for that in a moment, I promise. I'll make it all better." She could feel Jackson's stare on her, hot and heavy on her prickling skin, but she ignored him as best she could. She wasn't sure why she was so aware of him, but she didn't like it one bit.

Lucy focused on her patient instead. The wound had clotted, and though it didn't look infected, the kitten would need surgery to amputate the rest of the leg at the hip joint. First, though, she had to make sure the animal stayed stable enough to get an IV into him for fluids and antibiotics.

Straightening, Lucy met Jackson's gaze. "He's in decent condition for now, which is shocking given what you told me. If you hadn't come along when you did, I doubt the kitten would have survived much longer. His vitals are a little low, but good. If he's doing this well in a couple of hours, my colleague, Dr. Dave, whose office is just down the road, can do surgery to remove the rest of the leg. The kitten will then need to stay with me for a few more nights for monitoring."

Jackson frowned. "Why can't you do the surgery here?"

"Normally, I would, but with the hurricane coming, my supply shipment is delayed and I don't have some of the things I need." Lucy sighed. "Dr. Dave is very good. He was my mentor. He'll take good care of the kitten for you. And we have an agreement on the prices, because of the sanctuary."

"I don't care about the cost." Jackson rubbed his hand over the top of his short hair. "Do whatever you need to do to save him. I'll make it work."

The fact he cared so much about a creature he'd just found made Lucy's chest squeeze with something far too close to affection toward him. No. No, no, no. She didn't want to care about Jackson Durand. Been there. Done that. Had the emotional scars to prove it.

He shuffled his feet then shoved his hands

into the pockets of his jeans. "He'll be okay with three legs, right? I mean, humans do fine getting around, but I don't know much about—"

Lucy nodded. "He's young. He'll adapt. There'll be a healing period and adjustment involved, of course."

"Well, little guy. Looks like you're in the best possible hands. Yes, you are." Jackson stroked the kitten's head, and the little guy sure liked what he was doing. His tail limply thumped the table, and he watched Jackson with trusting eyes. A bond seemed to have formed already. Lucy had learned to trust her animals' intuition when it came to people, but there was still something about Jackson Durand that made her nervous. She didn't want to think too hard about why.

"Do you want to keep him afterward?" she asked him.

"Oh." Jackson looked up, seemingly startled by her question. "I don't… I'm not sure I should…" He took a deep breath. "With my work hours, I'm not home a lot." He frowned down at the kitten again. "I've never had a cat before, either. But I guess if no one else wants him, I could take him for a while. Like a foster situation."

"Do you want to name him then?"

"Oh. Um…"

She sighed. "You don't have to."

That line between his dark brows deepened for a second, then he tilted his head and smiled. "How about King? You know, because he has those stripes like a tiger?"

"Sure." Lucy got busy inserting an IV filled with warm saline to bring the kitten's temperature up slightly and started antibiotics. Then she drew some blood and ran a CBC to check platelets before checking her new patient's vitals again. The little guy took it in stride. Pleased the kitten was doing well, she pulled out her cell phone to call the neighboring clinic.

While Jackson looked around, she spoke with Dr. Dave.

"Hi. Yeah, I've got a surgical case for you. Kitten requiring an amputation. Can you work him in before the storm hits? Yes, he's stable. Okay. Great. I'll have him there in a bit. Thanks. 'Bye."

She tracked Jackson around the small space as she spoke to her colleague, unable to keep from taking in his tall, muscled form. He really was handsome. If you went for that type. Then again, Robert had been handsome, too, and look where that had gotten her. Trapped in a relationship where her fiancé, the man who was supposed to have her best interests at heart, had only loved her when she was totally dependent on him. Nope. Lucy had learned not to fall for pretty. No matter how charming and kind that package might be. To distract herself, she turned away to check on her new patient again, giving the kitten a scratch behind the ears and earning a mewl of happiness.

"King, are you ready to go see Dr. Dave? He'll take good care of you."

Two more mewls.

Lucy looked over at Jackson next, locking gazes with those mesmerizing eyes again. Her pulse tripped, and she swallowed hard. Seriously, she needed to get over that and quick. "My colleague can take him now if we can get King there soon." She stroked the kitten's back. "If you drive, I'll hold him and give you directions."

"Okay." Jackson smiled, and Lucy forgot to breathe. Dammit. Not good. Not good at all.

While Lucy went into the back with Dr. Dave, Jackson stood in the vet clinic trying to figure out exactly what the hell had possessed him to agree to foster a kitten—let alone one that would soon have three legs. He didn't know much about it but was pretty sure nursing King back to health would take a while, and he wasn't sure he'd have the time to commit to it, what with the current IC job and the cleanup efforts after Mathilda moved through. Then there was the regional director position. If he got the promotion, it would mean even more time away from home. And if he didn't get it, well…he didn't want to think about that. It was too important to him to fail. End of story.

Chest itching inside, he turned to inspect a rack full of dog toys and leashes, none of which would apply to his situation. Honestly, he was restless. Had been since he'd left the courthouse in Miami-Dade County, where he'd gone to pick up the results of his DNA testing. Not for a disease or anything like that. It was just one more effort to try to figure out who he really was and the identity of his birth mother. There was a woman there who specialized in tracking down hard-to-find people, so he thought he'd give it a try. After all these years, he probably should just leave it, not care anymore. His birth mom obviously hadn't, seeing as how she'd never tried to contact him in all this time.

Still, there was a hole inside him that nothing seemed to be able to fill, a gaping pit that he'd tried to patch on his own by always staying busy, always doing for others, like maybe that might improve his worthiness somehow. Prove he was worth keeping, worth staying around for...

Stupid, Jackson. So damned stupid.

He moved on down the wall to the cat toys. Brightly colored things with feathers and bells and squeakers. He picked up what looked like a stuffed mouse and jingled it near his ear. Silly thing.

Jackson placed it in a basket to buy then kept looking. He hadn't lied to Lucy. He worked a lot. Took on extra shifts. Not just for the overtime but for the experience. More hours logged looked good on his record and, hopefully, gave him a leg up when it came to promotion time.

Not an overachiever by nature, like Luis, Jackson still had ambitions—and that hole inside to fill—and at the moment he couldn't square a new pet with all that. Same way he couldn't quite square the calm, collected, curious Lucy he'd seen in her clinic just now with the fidgeting, flustered woman from the day before.

Sighing, Jackson moved on to the food. Wet, dry, mixed. He had no idea what a kitten that little would eat. Formula, maybe? He should probably ask Lucy. And yeah, he was going to keep it, at least for a while, because that's what he'd said he would do. And because he knew the pain of being left behind.

Besides, Jackson Durand never went back on his word.

Just then, an exam room door opened in the back and voices drifted out. Lucy and Dr. Dave, he assumed. The guy had seemed nice enough when she'd introduced them, his handshake solid and strong. He was maybe late fifties with the tanned, sun-weathered face of a true Conch.

Turning around, he spotted Lucy walking with Dr. Dave from the exam room, deep in conversation.

The first words that had popped into his mind yesterday when he'd met her had been *buttoned-up*, *locked down* and *repressed*. All sharp edges and nervous tics. Now, though, seeing her laughing and talking with Dr. Dave, the same way she'd been with her friend Stacy during the ERT meeting, had him shaking off an unwanted shock of awareness.

Or maybe that was exhaustion. Yesterday had ended three back-to-back twelve-hour shifts, and after today he was staring down another long run of another twenty-four hours on call, and that was even before Hurricane Mathilda arrived. Afterward there would be cleanup and rebuilding and...

Because, oh yeah, the National Weather Service had upgraded the tropical storm to hurricane status the night before. Which meant he'd then upgraded the readiness level of the ERT to two, with the trajectory of the storm altering slightly overnight and bringing it within closer range of the Keys. He needed to tell Lucy that as well.

His inner tension notched higher as she pointed toward him then smiled.

No. Stop it. He didn't want to be interested in Lucy Miller that way. Didn't want to think about her cute grin or how he'd gotten a whiff of her flowery, clean scent back at the clinic when they'd stood side by side at that exam table. And he especially didn't want to feel that warm, fuzzy feeling inside because she gave shelter to animals no one else wanted, like bald parrots or orphaned kittens.

She walked out now to join him at the counter. "Dr. Dave is going to start working on King now."

"Good." He paid the receptionist for the stuff in his basket then walked back out to his truck with Lucy. "How long will it take?"

"An hour, maybe two," she said as she opened the passenger side door of his old truck and climbed in. He walked around the front and got in behind the wheel then started the engine while she buckled her seat belt. "Dr. Dave will text me when it's over. And I'll pick him up for you tomorrow."

"Or," Jackson said, backing out of his spot, his arm across the seats as he peered over his shoulder. He did his best not to notice the fact his fingers had brushed against her bare shoulder when he'd done so, or how she'd shivered and pulled away from his touch. Lord, he needed to get his head in the game and out of fantasyland already. "We could grab a bite to eat while he's in surgery and I can see for myself how he does when it's over. You know, in case anything goes wrong."

He signaled then turned out of the lot back onto Palmetto Avenue, still berating himself for asking. God, what was up with him? The sooner he got out of here, the sooner he could get back to his houseboat and get some sleep. But there he was, asking her to lunch while heading south back to her place.

"Um…no. I'm not hungry." She frowned as she picked through the bag of things he'd bought for King. Her stomach rumbled loudly, and her scowl darkened.

Jackson gave her a side glance and a grin. "Liar."

"I can eat back at home."

"Or you could eat with me." He wasn't even sure why he was being so persistent about this, just that he wasn't ready to leave here yet. Because of the kitten. That's the excuse he was going with, anyway. "Come on. One meal. My treat."

Lucy looked like she wanted to argue, but he turned into the parking lot of a local beachside pub and cut the engine before she could stop him.

"Just lunch. That's all." He got out and walked around to open her door for her. "Please. It would make me feel better to see for myself King made it through the surgery all right. Then I'll go home."

She opened her mouth, closed it, then opened it again. Unbuckled her seat belt and finally got out, not looking at him. She was still dressed in baggy denim overalls, but she could've been wearing the crown jewels, given her queenly posture and rigid attitude. "Fine. One meal. And I can pay for myself."

"I'm sure you can." He closed the truck door after her and bit back a smile. "But I'm a gentleman and I invited you, so I'll pay."

"Really?" She gave him a quick side glance. "Stacy said you were a player."

Stunned, Jackson stood there blinking for a moment as Lucy walked away.

He needed to have a talk with Stacy, apparently.

Once they got inside, the hostess seated them at a table on the outside deck overlooking the marina. The air smelled of sea and deep-fried food with a touch of alcohol from the bar inside. The call of seagulls filled the air, and the silly birds landed on the railings and strutted on the deck, no qualms about begging for food. It was an atmosphere Jackson was familiar with, having grown up working in and around his parents' pub in Key West.

A server came by and took their drink order—iced tea for him and water with lemon for Lucy—then gave them menus before departing. He hid a smile as Lucy pulled a disinfectant wipe from her bag and wiped down her side of the table and her seat before thoroughly cleaning her menu. Then she rearranged the silverware and napkin before finally looking at the specials for the day.

"Know what you're going to have?" he asked, having decided on a grilled chicken salad himself.

Usually these oceanfront places were known for their seafood, but he'd been spoiled by his parents' Cuban recipes and had never found any others that compared, so he stuck with greens. He needed to eat something healthy anyway, after all the vending machine and cafeteria food he'd grabbed between runs.

Lucy frowned over at him from atop her menu. "I don't know. I've never been here before."

"Seriously? You live in Big Pine Key and you've never eaten at this place?"

"No." She shook her head and set the menu aside. "I usually cook at home. Or sometimes I order out and have food delivered, but always from the same place close to my house."

"Hmm." He was going to ask more, but the server arrived with their drinks and took their orders, interrupting him. Lucy ended up getting the same salad he did, minus the chicken and with the dressing and most of the toppings on the side. Basically, a bowl of plain lettuce with things she could put on herself. A mini salad bar. He waited while she fiddled with her glass and carefully removed the lemon wedge from the side, squeezing it into her water before placing it in her napkin and rolling it up into a tiny sealed packet then setting it in the far corner of the table. It was quite a production.

"So…" he said at last, breaking the awkward silence.

"So." Lucy blinked down at her hands in her lap. Finally, she sighed and looked up at him, her expression serious. "I have a condition."

"Sorry?" He sipped his tea and frowned, trying to catch up with her mind. He suspected he already knew what she was going to say but was surprised she'd just come out with it like that. Then again, bluntness could be a symptom of certain disorders like autism or OCD. Impulsivity, too. He tried to make light of it, as humor was always his fallback when things got too heavy. "Nothing fatal, I hope."

His joke fell flatter than her stare. "Obsessive-compulsive disorder."

"Oh. Okay." He sat back as the waitress delivered their salads. Nothing fancy, just a classic grilled chicken salad. Hard to go wrong there. He poured on his dressing while Lucy arranged her silverware yet again then set about picking through her food, removing anything that looked suspicious. Luis used to sort his candy by color because some of them were better than others, he said, but he'd gradually grown out of it as he'd gotten older, finding other, more socially acceptable outlets for that energy. Things like traveling abroad on mission trips to help the under-privileged.

Jackson started eating while she was still futzing with her lettuce. "That must be tough."

"It's fine. I've always been this way, so I've nothing to compare it to."

"I guess that's true." Jackson hailed the server for an extra napkin, waiting until they were alone again before continuing. "I noticed some tics at the meeting yesterday."

She froze. "What?"

"With your pens. Needing them in the right order. And when you walked down the hall, you didn't step on any cracks." He smiled. "Oh, and the tapping, with your fingers or your pen. Always in threes."

Her cheeks pinkened, and she swallowed hard. "How do you know about that?"

"I observe people. It's what I do. Plus, my brother has a mild case of Asperger's."

"Your brother?"

"Yeah. Dr. Luis Durand? I think you might know him from the hospital, or the meeting yesterday. Runs the ER at Key West General."

"Oh. Right. Yes, I know him," she said, glancing up at him. "You don't look anything like him."

"I'm handsomer." At his teasing, her cheeks got even redder if that were possible, and he quickly added, "I'm joking. Sorry. We're both adopted."

"Oh." Lucy took a small bite of salad, chewing slowly before swallowing. "You're a paramedic."

"Yep."

"And watching people is important in your job?" Her dubious tone made him chuckle.

"Of course." He ate another bite of salad, realizing it was actually better than he'd imagined. The creamy ranch dressing was homemade and garlicky without being overpowering. And the grilled chicken had a spicy coating, not quite Cajun, but close. The cool, crisp romaine was its perfect complement. "You can't properly treat a patient without understanding them. Medicine is about more than just diagnosing an illness."

She took that in a moment before going back to her salad sorting. "I suppose it is."

"Take your vet work, for example," Jackson went on. He probably should've just shut up, but for some reason he couldn't. Now that he had Lucy here and talking, he wanted to know more about her. Like a puzzle he needed to figure out. "When I brought King in today, you could've just stuck in an IV and taken him off to surgery, but you spent time comforting the little guy and getting to know him first. You established a connection."

Lucy gave a small flinch at that last word. Intrigued, he followed that trail farther.

"Must be hard, running a sanctuary. You must see all kinds of horrible things."

"Sometimes. But caring for those others have cast aside is also the most rewarding thing I've ever done. Those animals need me, and I won't let them down. I provide them with a better life, for whatever time they have left."

"Admirable. Really." He wiped his mouth then pushed his empty bowl aside, ignoring the zing of warmth her words had caused inside him. She was talking about animals, not people, being cast aside. *It's not about you, dude.* Considering their brisk interactions yesterday and today, she wouldn't care if Jackson got cast off a pier, let alone left behind by his birth mother. Not that he'd be telling her about that. He didn't share that with anyone.

"Must give you a sense of control, too," he said, desperate to get his errant thought back on track. "Running your own little universe on that compound."

Her astonished expression made him laugh, breaking his inner tension. His shoulders relaxed and he could breathe again. Jackson shrugged. "Like I said, I'm familiar with OCD and its side effects."

"Right." She ate a few more bites before speaking again. "The few times I've encountered Dr. Durand when I'm at the hospital visiting the children's ward, he always seems friendly and supportive of me and my therapy animals. He's a good man."

"The best I've ever met," Jackson said with

confidence. "And not just because he's my brother."

"Why?"

"Why what?"

"Why do you think he's the best man?" Lucy sipped of her water, narrowing her pretty brown eyes on him. "And you said you're adopted. What about your birth parents? Are they dead?"

"Wow." His brows rose. "Okay."

She blushed harder and lowered her gaze. "Sorry. I don't mean to blurt things out like that."

He chuckled. "It's...interesting. Nothing wrong with being blunt."

Lucy's frowned deepened. "Most people don't like it. Robert always used to keep me at home, away from people most times, because of it."

"Hmm." Jackson narrowed his gaze. "Well, I don't know this Robert guy, but he sounds terrible. And it's your lucky day, because I'm not most people." Jackson winked, enjoying how she got all flustered way more than he should.

What the hell am I doing? He had no business flirting with Lucy Miller. She obviously had a lot of stuff of her own to work through, and he wasn't looking to get involved with anyone, anyway. Flings, that's all he did these days. And from what he'd seen of her so far, Lucy was not the one-night-stand kind of gal.

He'd invited her to lunch because he'd needed to eat and to be polite. He should leave it at that.

Except something about her kept reeling him in closer, like a marlin on a hook. Kept drawing him deeper into curiosity about who she was and why she was the way she was, beyond her condition. Lucy Miller had walked into his life, quite literally, the day before, and that had to mean something. He didn't believe in coincidence. And he wasn't sure why exactly, but he felt compelled to find out.

"We should go," she said, pushing her half-finished plate away abruptly.

"You're not done eating yet." He sat back and crossed his arms. "And King's still got a ways to go before he's out of surgery. Plus, I'm your ride. I'll wait."

"Then I'll walk." She picked up a bread-stick and bit off the end. "I assure you, I'm used to being on my own."

"I'm sure you are." She'd mentioned this Robert guy, who'd kept her at home. He wasn't sure who the guy was or what his deal had been, but he didn't like him already. And as a man who kept his own distance from people, at least emotionally, he knew there was a story there, but he didn't want to push too hard. After all, this was one lunch, between people who'd go back to being strangers soon enough. Honestly, he should already be on his way back to Key West to wait on a text from her about the kitten. He could've used his day off to relax, catching up on some reading, maybe clean his houseboat.

None of that moved his butt out of the chair, though. "It's fine. I've got nowhere else to be."

Lucy kept chewing her breadstick, her sigh full of reluctant acceptance. "It doesn't bother you?"

"What?"

"My OCD?"

"Should it?" He'd grown up around Luis and worked around people with mental disorders all the time—nothing new there.

She shrugged. "Most people run the other way when they learn about my issues. Or else they feel like they need to take care of me. I'm not broken. I don't need to be fixed. I'm not an invalid."

"Understood." He snorted. "But did you ever consider that maybe they just want to help?"

"I don't need help, either." She gave him a steely look. "And I don't need your pity."

"I don't pity you."

"Good." She placed her napkin on the table then stood. "I'd like to go back to my compound now."

"Sure." Jackson paid the server then walked with her back out to his truck. The breeze had picked up, but it was still sunny and humid. More seagulls cried and swooped through the sky, looking for trash people had dropped. Another perfect day in paradise. Hard to believe this could all change soon when the storm moved in.

The short drive back to her place was quiet, until he pulled up at the rear of her compound, instead of the main gate. It was the way he'd come in earlier, too.

"Thank you for lunch," Lucy said, clambering out of the truck. "I'll text you with an update as soon as King comes out of surgery." She pulled out her phone. "What's your number?"

"My number's listed on the team contact page of the binder I dropped off earlier."

"Got it." Lucy started to close the door, but Jackson stopped her.

"Hey. I need to let you know, we moved to readiness level two today."

"And that means what?" she asked, peeking back into the truck at him.

"Read the binder," he said, grinning. "If we get to level one, you'll need to come into Key West for the duration. I don't expect things to get that bad, though. All the forecasts are currently taking Mathilda well past the Keys, so we should just get a brush of the outer bands at the most. Rain and a bit of wind. That's about it." He hiked his chin. "And thanks for taking care of King. I'll wait for your text."

CHAPTER FOUR

"HEY, CAROL. HOW are you doing? You look great," Jackson said the following Friday. The retirement village where the woman and her husband lived on Key West was a frequent stop for the EMTs. He set his med pack on the floor of their small, tidy condo and crouched by the lady's bedside. "Why are we here today?"

"She ate kung pao something or other," her husband, Vic, said from his rocking chair in the corner. "Told her not to touch that stuff."

"Eh…" Carol waved dismissively at her husband. "Get outta here."

Her Bronx accent was strong today, and Jackson bit back a grin. "You know all that salt will get you every time with your high blood pressure, Carol."

She gave him a pouty look. "I didn't have that much."

"Well, in your case, with your heart problems, any amount is too much," Ned chimed in from the other side of the bed, where he was getting out a cuff and stethoscope to check her vitals. He gave Jackson a side look then grinned. "I think you just wanted to see us again."

"You're not wrong." The older lady shot Jackson a sly smile. "Why aren't you guys married yet? Are you and he a couple?"

"What?" Jackson shook his head. "No. I'm not gay. Neither is Ned, that I know of. Not that there's anything wrong with that."

"Of course there's not," Vic said, his chair squeaking as he rocked slowly. "Our son's gay."

"Pressure's high. One eighty over one hundred," Ned said, pulling out his earpieces, then pressed a finger to each of her swollen ankles. "Two-plus pitting edema bilateral lower extremities." He looked up at Carol. "You're going to need a shot of Lasix, honey. Same as before. You're retaining fluids again because of all the salt in that food."

She sighed. "Fine. I know what that medication is. You don't have to tell me."

"Don't get mad at us," Jackson said, drawing up the injection. The diuretic would help flush out her system. Her attitude, however, was here to stay. He hoped that if he was blessed enough to reach the ripe old age of eighty-eight, like Carol, he'd be that feisty, too. He glanced over at her husband, Vic, as he tapped the syringe to get the air bubbles out. "Whose idea was it to get the food?"

Vic shrugged. "Hers, but I don't blame her. I mean, you have to indulge once in a while, right? Life's too short."

"True." Jackson finished drawing up her meds then grabbed an alcohol pad to clean Carol's arm before giving her the injection. When he was done, he shoved the used needle into a portable red biohazard container then stripped off his gloves before putting a bandage on her arm. "How long have you guys been married again?"

"Fifty-nine years," Carol said.

"Seems twice as long," Vic said.

"Shut up, you." Carol rolled slightly to give

him a look over her shoulder, but her smile was indulgent. She turned back to Jackson again.

"Well, it's good this happened now and not tomorrow," Jackson said. "You guys ready for the hurricane?"

"We are." Vic stood and walked over to his wife's bedside and took her hand. "They're moving us all into the clubhouse later today for safety reasons."

"Good." He finished shoving his equipment back into his pack then joined Ned at the end of Carol's bed. "Make sure you take all those warnings seriously, okay? This storm is nothing to play around with, understand?"

"Yes, sir," Carol said, winking at him. "You're sexy when you take control."

Jackson chuckled and shook his head. "You just don't quit, do you?"

"No, sir." She squeezed Vic's hand. "That's the secret to our longevity."

He and Ned let themselves out, then headed back to Key West General. By the time they got there, it was early afternoon. Jackson found Luis in the ER, staring at some CT images on a computer screen at the nurses' station.

"Those of the motorcycle accident victim we brought in last week?" Jackson asked, checking out the scans of a badly fractured pelvis.

"Yes." Luis scrolled through several more images then clicked off the computer. "He's doing much better, according to the last report I got from the ortho surgeon. Took four hours of surgery to repair all the damage. They're going to evaluate his leg today."

"That's tough, man. I know when we picked him up from the scene, there was a lot of gravel and denim and bits of bone we had to debride from the wound. I hope they can save it." Jackson followed his brother out of the ER and down the hall toward the conference room, where an emergency ERT meeting had been called. In true hurricane form, Mathilda wasn't playing by the rules and had adjusted course yet again. Jackson had spent his time between runs deciding whether or not to raise the readiness level to one and had just come to a conclusion about five minutes prior.

"Me too." Luis held the door for him as they walked into the already-full conference room. "They applied a fixation device yesterday to Reed's leg, but he still has no pulse in his left foot, so there's been some compromised blood flow and possible nerve damage. His life's more secure at this point, but the future of that leg is in doubt. As soon as this meeting's over, I'm going upstairs for another update."

He nodded then walked up to the podium while Luis searched the room for an empty seat. Jackson kept his gaze straight ahead, determined not to seek out Lucy. Nope. He'd spent more than enough time texting back and forth with her over the last week about King. Not to mention how his thoughts kept returning to her during the night, too. She was interesting and she was taking care of King, that was all. And maybe if he told himself that enough times, he'd believe it.

Luis took a seat next to Stacy Williams and looked about as comfortable as a turkey on

Thanksgiving, but Jackson didn't have time to think about why that was. Today was all about the coming storm and making sure they were ready.

"Right. Let's get started, then," he said. "Thanks, everyone, for coming on such short notice. We've got a lot of new information to cover today, so best get to it."

Jackson waited for the hushed murmurs to die down then jumped right in. "Unfortunately, the news I have today isn't good. Based on the latest forecast models from the National Weather Service, Mathilda is expected to strengthen to a category four storm by tomorrow morning, and though it won't make direct landfall in the Keys, we are expecting the outer bands to cause significant storm surge and wind damage throughout the area as it passes by. Therefore, I'm raising our readiness level to one, effective midnight tonight. You all know how this goes and should have been expecting it."

"Tomorrow morning?" Luis said, scowling. "That's much sooner than originally expected. I thought it wouldn't hit until to-morrow evening at the soonest."

"Like I said, things have changed fast." He took a deep breath. "And given the hurricane's current speed and trajectory, once it hits the Gulf of Mexico and the warmer waters there, it's going to be a monster. So, I've already put out bulletins to the local media, per our ERT protocol, and everyone on the team quarantines in Key West until after Mathilda passes. All top-level protocols are now in place and emergency services mobilized. We are warning residents in the Keys to evacuate to the mainland now or find lodging within Key West proper for the duration of the event. Any questions?"

A flurry of hands went into the air, and Jackson patiently answered them all until everyone was satisfied. Surprisingly, there were no objections. He'd thought for sure Lucy, at least, would have protested. Finally, after the meeting was adjourned and all the team members went off to brief their respective groups, Jackson made his way over to where

Luis sat beside Stacy. Neither of them looked happy.

"Everything okay?" he asked, coming up to them.

"Not really," Stacy said, rubbing her crossed arms. "Lucy isn't here today. I even said I'd pick her up and drive her in, but she refuses to leave her compound."

Jackson's stomach plummeted to his toes. Guess that explained her lack of protest. "I'll call her and talk to her about it."

"I don't think it will do any good," Stacy said, her expression concerned. "She's determined to stay there and ride this thing out, but I think this one's going to be bad, Jackson. She's tough, but not that tough."

"No. You're right. She can't stay there by herself." Jackson scowled. "It's too dangerous."

"Well, good luck getting her to budge, brother," Luis said, scrubbing a hand over his face. "All she has to do is not answer her phone. People do what they want and what they think is best, no matter the danger or whom they hurt in the process, even themselves."

At that last part Stacy gave a pained gasp, and Jackson's instincts went on high alert. Yeah, there was definitely something going on there. But he didn't have time to ask about it. Not with Lucy's life on the line. Instead, he took out his phone and tried to call. No answer. He fired off a quick text next then waited. No reply.

Previously, she'd always answered right away, even if it was just a curt, one-word response.

Dammit.

Luis was right. She was avoiding him, and now was definitely not the time to do that. Not with preparations for the incoming Mathilda barreling down on them at warp speed and people's lives and his future at stake. But more than anything he was worried about Lucy, picturing her stranded all alone out there on Big Pine Key, possibly hurt or worse.

Then his phone buzzed, and hope flared to life.

Only to be quickly doused. It wasn't Lucy. It was Ned letting him know another call had come in. He was on duty until nine o'clock tonight. The muscles between his shoulder blades knotted tighter. "Stacy, go ahead and brief your departments. I'll handle Lucy. Don't worry."

Jackson waited until she was gone, then turned to his brother. "Can you take over IC for me tonight after my shift ends?"

"What? Why?" Luis frowned. "You aren't going to do anything reckless, are you?"

"No." *Yes.* Maybe. They made their way back toward the ER and the ambulance bay. "I can't leave Lucy out there by herself." He stopped and rubbed his hand over the top of his short hair. "Look, the level one doesn't go into effect until midnight. If I drive out to Big Pine Key after my shift at nine, I'm sure I can get her and get back to Key West in plenty of time."

Luis gave him a look. "That's cutting it awfully close. No. I don't like it, Jackson."

"Well, good thing it's not up to you, then." He dug in his heels. The brothers rarely fought, but when they did, it was usually over a matter of principle. "Look, I'm the one taking the risk here, okay? And I'm fine doing it." At his brother's dubious stare, Jackson's anger spiked, more at himself than anyone. *Fine. Whatever.* "Stop glaring at me like that. Really, it's fine. And this has nothing to do with sex, if that's what you're thinking. Lucy barely tolerates me. But as IC, I can't just leave her out there to die, can I? Besides, she's disobeying my orders already by not being at the meeting. If I let her continue to do that, I won't be seen as an effective leader, will I? So yeah. I'm going out there to get her."

"So, this is about the promotion then?" Luis asked, sounding thoroughly unconvinced.

"Of course it is," Jackson said, throwing up his hands. "What else would it be about?"

Luis gave him a too-perceptive stare for a moment, then sighed. "I just hope you know what you're doing, brother."

Me too. "Keep an eye on your phone tonight. I'll text you if there are any problems."

With that he turned and walked out of

Key West General ER and headed toward the waiting ambulance, wondering himself just exactly what the hell he was doing, but knowing it was already too late to change his mind. The decision had been made for him anyway, the second Lucy had chosen to stay home rather than attend the meeting this afternoon.

He'd rescue her come hell or high water. And given the severity of the storm approaching, it would most likely be both.

One of the reasons Lucy had bought the compound was its isolation. She liked her solitude. And if she got lonely, she had her animals to keep her company. Usually. Now, she'd had Dr. Dave take them all to Miami with him and his partner for the duration of the storm. Well, most of them, anyway. The only ones left were Sam, who never left her side, Bubba, King and Mitzi.

Mitzi Gator never left. Just like Lucy.

She parked her car outside the front gate and let herself into the yard where the pregnant three-legged alligator lived in the pond on the far corner of the property. She was currently feasting on what looked like a seagull she must've caught. Normally, Lucy would've moved the reptile to a specialized place for her kind, but Mitzi had been a resident here since Lucy had moved in, and she didn't want to send the grumpy gal away until after her eggs had hatched, which, according to the calendar in the clinic, wouldn't be until after the storm. Not great timing, but nothing to do about it.

One more reason why Lucy couldn't leave. Mitzi might need help, and she refused to abandon her.

She locked the gate behind her then walked the far perimeter toward the front door of her vintage two-story house. The place had been built sixty years ago and needed some repairs, but overall it was cozy and livable and inviting. Just what she wanted in a home.

Sam met her at the door, tail wagging and tongue lolling. She crouched to give him a good scratch behind the ears. "There's my baby," she cooed, kissing his furry snout. "How's my handsome boy doing, huh? Are you a good boy? Yes, you are. Sammy's such a good boy."

The skies had grown darker by the hour and the palm trees stood out in stark contrast, sending a blot of alarm through her gut. But Lucy had worked hard to get here. She'd be damned if she'd let a storm chase her out of it now, even one as fierce as Mathilda was predicted to be. She tossed her keys on a side table in the living room then headed for the kitchen, where she sat at the table to make a list of everything she needed to do by nightfall, while Sam curled up at her feet with his favorite squeaky toy.

First there was installing the metal shutters over the wind-resistant windows. Then there was barring the fiberglass exterior doors and the heavy-duty metal door on the garage and the clinic supply area out back. All of it should keep her property protected against up to 140-mile-per-hour winds. According to the last weather report she'd heard on the way back here from the big box supply store, Mathilda's maximum sustained winds weren't expected to exceed 130, so she should be fine.

Plus, she had the basement. Which was where she headed next, to check her supplies. A planner by nature, Lucy kept well stocked on items she might need for both herself and any of her patients. But her OCD added another layer so, in addition to the usual water and canned goods, she also had plenty of other things, too, like a large cooler and lots of battery-powered lanterns, along with boxes of nonperishable foods she'd ordered in case of an emergency. She wasn't a prepper but could probably give one a run for their money.

She rearranged things by pushing the supplies against one wall to clear space for King's and Bubba's cages. Sam's, too. Mitzi would have to make it on her own for now, since there definitely wasn't enough room for her down here, not that Lucy would even try.

"What do you think, Sammy?" she asked the dog, who was sniffing everything in sight. "We'll bring your bed down here, too. And your food and your water. We'll be just fine, won't we?"

The dog looked up at her and whined, his ears back like he was worried.

Or hungry. Lucy checked her watch. Damn. It was after six now and way past Sammy's dinnertime. "Come on, boy. Let's get you something to eat, huh?"

They went back upstairs, and she filled his bowl before checking her phone for messages. Lucy frowned, seeing three from Jackson, which she quickly scrolled past, and one from Dr. Dave.

She hit redial on the vet's number then leaned her hips against the edge of the counter, waiting for him to pick up.

"Hey, Lucy," Dr. Dave said over the sound of a radio in the background. "Thanks for calling me back."

"Sure. Where are you?"

"Todd and I are getting ready to head to the mainland. When are you leaving?"

"I'm not." Lucy frowned. "Mathilda's supposed to brush past us. I'm staying here, in the basement."

"I don't think that's a good idea, Lucy," Dr. Dave warned. "I've been down here through a lot of hurricanes, and I don't like the track of this one. With the speed constantly changing, it could get rough. We're leaving in about an hour to drive north. You're free to go with us if you want. We've got room."

"No," she said, firmly. She loved her mentor, but she wasn't about to budge. She couldn't. If she lost this place, she wasn't sure what she'd do. "I've got provisions, and I'm prepared to ride it out."

"Are you sure?"

"I am." She straightened and bent to pick up Sam's now empty food bowl. "Be safe."

"You too," Dr. Dave said. "And if you change your mind, Lucy, the news said Key residents could hunker down in Key West. Go sooner rather than later."

After letting Sam out to go potty and cleaning his dishes, she went back outside to make sure the clinic was secure and bring in the last of the supplies she'd bought today from her car. The sky had turned a weird greenish-gray color, whether from the approaching storm or from evening setting in, she didn't know. Either way, her adrenaline spiked, and her sense of urgency notched higher. Once she'd finished at the clinic, she battened down anything that might blow away in the storm then went to pull out the metal shutters from the storage shed in back to start fixing them into place on the windows. She set the ladder up to start on the upper floors first. An hour later, those were done and Lucy started on the lower level just as the first raindrops fell.

Huh... According to her watch, it wasn't quite 9:00 p.m. yet, but given how the winds had picked up, Mathilda's outer bands might arrive earlier than expected. She worked methodically around the house until she reached the last window, this one on her office. Sam alternated between circling her ankles nervously and barking at the leaves rustling in the wind. Hot and thirsty, she went inside for a drink and had just gotten a bottled water out of the fridge when her cell phone rang, the perky tune at direct odds with the ominous weather outside.

She gulped her water and frowned at the caller ID. Jackson. Again.

Part of her said to ignore it. Let it go to voice mail again. Except he'd left six messages already. Dammit. She answered bluntly. "I'm not leaving."

"I'm on my way to get you," he said, ignoring her statement.

"Like hell you are." Sam barked, and she gave the dog a stern *Be quiet* look. "Stay where you are, Jackson. I'm fine. We're going to hunker down in the basement. There's food and water, and I've already moved the animals down there, including King. He's doing fine, by the way."

"I'm glad to hear the kitten's good, but the storm's getting stronger, Lucy." The alarm in his voice ratcheted her own anxiety higher, but she tamped it down as best she could. "I'm not leaving you there alone."

"It's not your choice to make." She'd been down that road of people thinking she couldn't do for herself. She refused to go back to being powerless again. "I'm fine. Seriously. And what about your team? You need to stay in Key West to oversee everything. Stay there. I'm not your problem."

"You've been nothing but my problem since the day we met." His voice sounded exasperated. "You disobeyed orders by not showing up at the meeting today, and you're disobeying now. I'll be there shortly. This isn't up for debate, Lucy."

"You're right. It isn't." She ended the call before he could respond. God. She might sound crazy, but she needed to do this. Why couldn't anyone understand that? She needed to stand on her own, prove she could handle this. For herself and for anyone else who'd ever doubted her abilities. She wasn't helpless. She could do this. She would do this.

Then a gust of wind howled around the corner of the house, and the ladder outside her office window teetered precariously before settling back into place. Sam barked, running to the basement door then back to the kitchen as if urging her to go. Now.

Fight or flight pounded through her system, causing her anxiety and OCD to flare supernova bright, but Lucy refused to be scared off. She bent to reassure Sam, who seemed less certain about their predicament. "We can do this, boy. Yes, we can."

There was one more shutter to install, then she'd head to the basement with Sam. She stared out through the screened-in porch only to stop and stare at the mess of leaves covering the floor. She'd swept the whole place up earlier. Cursing under her breath, she grabbed the broom and pushed them all into the corner. Then she headed outside and around the corner, only to get distracted by Mitzi at the pond. She should make one more check of the egg mound before hunkering down for the night. Oh, and the garage. Better move her car in there and lock it up tight. She turned to do that, then halted. Did she lock the front door? She couldn't remember now…

Focus, Lucy. Focus.

Right. The last storm shutter. She headed in that direction. Except when she got there, the force of the gusts made picking up the heavy piece of sheet metal harder than she'd expected. Then the stupid ladder blew over and smashed one of her planters, scattering ceramic shards and potting soil everywhere. Now she needed to clean that up, too.

You can do this. You're in control.

But her usual mantra only went so far as conditions worsened and things spiraled more and more out of control...

"Go inside," she said to Sam who'd remained steadfastly by her side through it all. When it became obvious that he wouldn't budge without her, she finally relented. "Okay. Come on."

She'd worry about getting that last shutter on later. For now, she needed to take her meds and hope for a good dose of luck.

CHAPTER FIVE

"DAMMIT!" JACKSON SHOUTED as wind screamed in his ears and a burning pain sliced across his thigh.

The moment he'd caught sight of the dark shape hurtling toward him, he'd acted on instinct and leaped into a diving roll. But the fierce gales blowing in off the ocean slowed his movements enough to allow the claw of the large alligator to snag the leg of his paramedic uniform pants…and his flesh. He came swiftly to his feet, ignoring the heat shooting up his thigh from the wound. Eyes trained on the animal, he dropped into a crouch. It looked huge, easily ninety to a hundred pounds, but Jackson had a hard time getting past its mouth—wide-open and lined with vicious teeth.

"Why couldn't you stick to puppies and kittens, Lucy?" he muttered as he took a slow step back. The gator remained still, but that open mouth and the speed with which the thing had overtaken him earlier made him more than a little wary.

When he was a good twenty feet away, he carefully straightened, keeping his gaze steady on his target. "There's a good alligator."

After that last phone call, Lucy's obstinate refusal to leave had blared through his head like a clarion call. Of all the stubborn, stupid decisions to make... No. Issues or not, he was taking control. She had no idea what they might be up against, but he'd been through enough hurricanes to know never to underestimate one. She might not want to go, but he intended to cart her out of there by any means necessary. Or, at least he had, until the gator showed up.

He straightened a bit more and took another step back. The gator across from him maintained its aggressive stance. A true standoff. Well, if he was going down, it would be fighting.

Then, out of nowhere, a heavy weight blindsided him and dropped him to the ground.

Jackson hit hard on his chest, but quickly regained his senses. His first thought was another gator had nailed him from behind, but no. Those were human hands gripping his shoulders. A quick glance across the yard showed the gator had backed away, as if unsure what to make of this new intruder. He flipped over fast and pinned his assailant beneath him, only to realize it was Lucy.

"What the hell are you doing?" he yelled, partly to be heard over the howling wind and partly out of sheer frustration. She peered up at him, eyes dark and wide through the wet hair covering her face. Gradually, he also became aware of her petite frame and the press of her breasts against his chest, his senses heightened because of the storm raging around them.

She shoved hard at him, but he didn't budge. At least not until her fist hit the wound in his thigh where the gator had scratched him, then he cursed loudly. Hot, searing pain bolted straight to his brain, and Jackson pinned her hands above her head, the move bringing their faces inches apart.

"Answer me, Lucy! What the hell are you doing out here?"

She stared up at him, her gaze sparkling with defiance, and for a second he got lost.

"I could ask you the same thing," she growled, struggling under him. "I told you not to come."

That stubborn, tenacious tilt to her jaw was back, along with the sense he got of her vulnerability underlying it all. The enduring essence of battles fought. Some won. Too many lost. He recognized her grit, because he saw the same thing when he stared in the mirror every day.

Jackson lifted his weight off her and stood, pulling her up with him as he went. He paused to glance over at the alligator, but the darkness and the storm made it difficult to see.

"Did you hurt Mitzi?" she yelled over the wind.

"Who?"

"Mitzi, the alligator. Is she hurt?" She yanked free and raced across the yard toward the pond.

"The thing could've killed me," he roared, chasing after her. His words were swallowed by the wind. They kept running. Swearing under his breath, Jackson ignored the daggers in his thigh as he closed the distance. Finally, she slowed near a thicket of palm trees. Through the waving fronds, he made out the hulking shape of the beast as it cowered near a huge pile of earth, leaves and twigs.

"Lucy!"

She spun around, her expression a mix of concern and anger. "What?"

His patience unraveled, mainly because she seemed more concerned about that alligator than her own well-being. That was the last straw. "We need to go now before conditions get worse."

"I told you I'm not leaving." She looked away, squinting into the thicket.

"I don't have time for this," Jackson shouted.

"Neither do I. Go. Don't let me stop you. You shouldn't have come to begin with. I told you that."

Yep. She had. And if he'd been a different person, he might've listened. But as it was, Jackson couldn't leave. His honor and instincts wouldn't let him. She might not care about herself, but he did. It was his job to care.

Determined to end this, he closed the short space between them and grabbed her arm, thinking he'd pick her up and toss her over his shoulder to cart her away. Except no sooner had he reached her than Sam ran up to them, wet and bedraggled and barking like crazy. One more thing to worry about. Fine. Instead of the truck, Jackson pulled Lucy toward the house, the dog nipping at his heels as fresh jolts of pain shot from his injured leg. "We're leaving. Now. Grab the animals and anything else you need and let's go."

He was used to taking charge often enough in his job as an EMT—surely he could handle one pissed-off woman. At least that's what he'd thought, until Lucy dug in her heels and tugged hard, making him stumble and sending a fresh zing of agony up his leg. "Lucy, stop—"

"No! You stop!" she yelled. "This is my property and you're trespassing."

"I'm trying to help you," he yelled back, wondering how his efforts had gone so horribly awry.

"I told you I don't need your help!"

Any other time he'd have said fine. Let her do what she wanted. But now there was a hurricane about to slam into this place, and he'd sworn an oath to save and protect, and dammit.

He couldn't leave her here alone. He knew all too well what that was like.

"Can we at least go inside and discuss this?" he shouted back, and turned toward the front door.

She stayed put, making him drag her awkwardly for several feet. "I don't want you here." When he didn't slow down, she tugged again and yelled even louder. "Go away! I don't need you! I don't need anybody!"

The fraying tether on his patience snapped and Jackson whirled around fast and she smacked into his chest. He bent and shouted right near her ear so there was no doubt she heard him. "Too bad. I'm here and I'm not going anywhere until you're in the truck with me. Now, we can do this easy or hard, but either way, you and your animals are coming to Key West. Which will it be?"

She glared at him, not the least bit intimidated. Under different circumstances, he'd have admired that. "Last time I checked, this was still a free country."

"There's a difference between freedom and stupidity. Now move it." He dragged her toward the porch, not realizing until he was halfway up the stoop that the front door had been blocked off with a galvanized steel sheet. Cursing, he backtracked to the gravel pathway around the side of the house and noticed the same measures had been taken with the windows.

Good for her. Bad for him.

Dammit. There had to be a way in, since she'd gotten out.

"Let. Me. Go!" Lucy tried again.

He spotted a small screened-in porch and headed that way, going straight through and not stopping until they were standing in her kitchen. Then he slammed the door shut behind them, muting the howling wind. His ears rang with the sudden lack of noise. "You have five minutes to grab your things while I get the animals. Where are they?" He let go of her at last. "I'll turn off your utilities on the way, too, if you tell me where the fuse box and valves are."

When she didn't move right away, he thought maybe she was in shock. He'd seen it happen under far less stressful conditions. But a quick visual assessment of her showed no signs. No rapid breathing. No dilated pupils. No pale skin. In fact, her cheeks were pink, and her eyes sparkled with rage.

"I told you, I'm not—" she started.

Jackson looked at his watch, a muscle ticking near his jaw. "Four minutes, thirty seconds."

"Leaving," she finished, tapping the toe of her sneaker against the tile floor.

Lord Almighty, why was she making this so difficult? He knew her OCD probably had something to do with it, but he was one of the good guys, or at least he tried to be. So why then, as he stood there, leg throbbing and pride hurt, did he feel like *he* should apologize?

That was stupid. He had nothing to apologize for. This was a matter of life or death. He couldn't leave her here. End of story.

They stared at each other, at an impasse, just like before with the gator. Except Jackson feared Lucy could be just as dangerous to him in a different way. Yes, she was six inches shorter than his six-two height and barely a hundred and thirty pounds soaking wet. Physically, it should've been an easy fight for him to win. Mentally and emotionally? Well, the more time he spent with her, the more difficult it proved to be.

"I appreciate you coming all this way. I do. But I'm not leaving, Jackson. I can't." Her quiet response caught him off guard.

"Why? Why can't you leave? Are you agoraphobic, too?" It made sense, as the anxiety and phobias went hand in hand with her OCD. But property could be replaced. Lives couldn't.

"Why do you care?" she countered, then held up her hand before he could answer.

"Never mind. Look, I get that you think you need to swoop in here like some superhero and save the day. But your time would be better spent as IC, with your team helping people in Key West who need to be rescued."

Her voice had taken on a slow, soothing quality, the same one she'd used with the injured kitten he'd brought into the clinic. The same one he used with patients in emergencies. King had responded well and done what she'd wanted. Too bad it wouldn't work on him.

"Time's up." He showed her the glowing dial of his smart watch then sidled past her down the hall to what he assumed was the basement door, based on the meows and squawks echoing from below. "I'm going to get those cages and load them in my truck." He grabbed a plastic bag off the counter and thrust it into her hands. "Pack up what you want of your stuff. Last chance."

"You can't just come in here and take over," Lucy yelled from behind him.

"Already did," Jackson called back as he

descended the wooden stairs to the basement. At the bottom, he stopped and scanned the space. King's cage was in the corner. The kitten meowed loudly when it saw him and licked his finger through the bars. Jackson smiled despite the situation. "Hey, little man."

The kitten's back area where they'd removed the leg was still wrapped in thick bandages, and an IV tube ran from his front leg to a bag hung up on one side of the cage. Getting all this upstairs alone was going to more difficult than he'd first imagined. In the opposite corner was Bubba, dancing furiously back and forth across his perch, screeching song lyrics and tossing food out of his bowl all over the floor with his beak.

Yeah. Maybe too difficult.

With a sigh, Jackson straightened and made his way back up to find Lucy. It was harder to see now, since the sun was hidden by thick storm clouds and steel shutters covered the windows, so he flipped on the lights. The living room at one end of the hall was neat and tidy, as expected, but impersonal. No pictures or personal touches at all. Same with the kitchen.

He checked another open doorway across the corridor and found her office. Again, clean and impersonal. Hardwood floors, minimal furniture. The only splashes of color were a watercolor painting of a sunset hanging on the wall and a stained-glass lamp on the desk. With her OCD, he shouldn't have expected a bunch of knickknacks, but still it felt odd. No connections, no memories, no ties to her past.

Jackson started to walk to the hall again and bumped into a file cabinet. Something tumbled off the top and hit the floor. He picked it up, hissing slightly as his injured thigh protested. A picture frame. Huh... He turned it over to reveal a photo of a younger Lucy with a man holding her from behind, his arms wrapped around her middle and his chin resting on her shoulder. They were both grinning and Lucy had on an engagement ring. *Hello, Robert.*

Bang!

The wind snapped a tree branch against the side of the house, jarring him back to reality. That was the strongest gust yet. And now hard rain pelted the house. Yep. The outer bands were getting close. Too close.

Time to go. Now.

He tucked the frame under his arm and hobbled for the stairs up to the second floor.

"Hey, Lucy?" he called up. "I need your help with—"

Booming thunder and cracking lightning cut him off.

Dammit.

They could make a run for it on the Overseas Highway. It was only thirty miles back to Key West, but man, he really didn't want to get caught out there in the middle of the hurricane. No way they'd survive. Which meant staying put was the best bet. Except hunkering down here meant he had to let Luis know he had to continue as IC until the storm passed. It was the last thing he wanted to do, but the only choice he had for now.

He pulled out his phone and texted Luis

then shoved the device back in his pocket with a decisive nod and went to find Lucy. "Looks like neither one of us is going anywhere for a while."

CHAPTER SIX

"WHAT?" ANXIETY KNOTTED tighter in Lucy's gut. He couldn't mean... The thought of being stuck with Jackson Durand for the duration of the storm was almost enough to make her wish she'd evacuated.

Almost.

She raised her chin and crossed her arms to hide the trembling in her limbs.

You can do this. You're in control.

Except the harder she fought her OCD urges, the more they wanted to come out until she couldn't stop herself from tapping her foot on the floor.

One, two, three. One, two, three. One, two, three.

The fact he stood there watching her didn't help. Honestly, his too-perceptive gaze unnerved her more than the hurricane outside. Another loud crack outside the still-uncovered office window had her running to see huge limbs from an oak tree across the compound snap off like dry twigs and made her throat dry. "We need to get in the basement. Now."

"Agreed. But we need to cut the utilities first. And get that last shutter on the window there."

Right. Tasks were good. Tasks kept her focused.

"I'll get the shutter." Lucy rushed toward the kitchen door. "It can be tricky getting them into the tracks."

He stopped her, the air between them crackling with tension. "I'll get the shutter. You stay inside and cut the utilities. Where's the metal sheet?"

Rather than waste any more valuable time, she pointed toward the kitchen. "Near the back porch."

"Flashlight?"

"In the box on the counter. There's also battery-operated lanterns, extra batteries and some small propane tanks."

He headed down the hall to the kitchen, and

she stared after him, the reflective letters on the back of his EMT shirt highlighting the V between his broad shoulders and narrow waist. For reasons she didn't want to think about too much at present, Jackson seemed even rougher, tougher, more masculine than usual, and deep in her core there was a fluttering response.

"Lucy," he called, dragging her out of her inappropriate thoughts. "Come take one of these lanterns to use after you shut off the power."

She did as he asked, the heavy silence between them filled by her pulse pounding loud in her ears.

"Be sure to fill the tubs and sinks before you shut off the water," he said before heading out the back door.

"Already done," she said to no one but herself. Her stomach went into free fall at the thought of being stuck together with him through the hurricane. Memories of being trapped in a home with Robert, him not allowing her to do anything for herself, him always telling her he knew best, him smothering her with his good intentions until she'd been all but unable to do for herself.

She couldn't go back there. Couldn't let that happen again. Couldn't depend on Jackson, no matter how much her aching heart might want to. Down that path was insanity.

The loud thwack of the screen door slamming against its frame startled her out of her paralysis.

Utilities. Right. She headed to the closet, lantern in hand, to shut off the power and water.

By the time she got back to the kitchen, Jackson had returned, his body silhouetted in the doorway by the black skies behind him. A muscle ticked near his tense jaw, and his high cheekbones stood out in sharp relief, making him look almost feral.

He gripped either side of the door frame, as if he might be sucked back out into the storm, and mumbled something she couldn't hear over the roar of the wind. Lucy moved closer, hoping to pull him inside before the door blew off its hinges. "What?"

"I can't," he shouted, tightening his grip on the wall.

She scowled. "Can't what?"

He slumped and would have crumpled to the ground if she hadn't wedged herself between him and the wall. His muscled weight nearly squashed her as she struggled to keep upright. "What's wrong? What happened? Are you hurt?"

"Gotta...close...the door," he rasped near her ear.

Lucy wrapped her arm around his waist and braced herself, feeling sticky warm blood on her hip. *Oh no.* Her chest constricted, and her veins tingled from excess adrenaline. None of this had gone the way she'd hoped, but she had to pull it together for Jackson.

You can do this. You're in control.

She glanced down at the long gash in his pants. The dark material made it hard to tell, but based on his weakness, she'd guess he'd lost some blood. Switching into vet mode, she began treating him like one of her animal patients and guided him toward the kitchen table. "You're going to be okay."

They barely made it before his knees buckled. Jackson fell across the table, facedown, and groaned. Lucy stumbled into one of the chairs, managing to catch herself before she tumbled to the floor. Then she scrambled back up and ran to the door, shoving hard against the fierce gusts. Once the latch clicked into place, she turned the dead bolt then raced back to the table.

"Jackson?" She grabbed a chair and turned it at an angle. He grunted. "Can you roll to your right? I'll hold the chair and you can slide into it and leave your injured leg straight in front of you."

Slowly, he did as she asked. Once he was in the chair, his head fell back, his eyes tightly shut.

She leaned over him. "Jackson?"

He opened one eye. "What happened?"

"Mitzi the gator."

"Mitzi Gaynor?" Jackson frowned. "Isn't that some lounge singer from Vegas?"

Lucy bit back a nervous laugh. Dr. Dave and his partner had named the alligator before Lucy had arrived. The fact Jackson recognized the gator's celebrity namesake made her like him a little more, against her will.

She checked his pulse to distract herself. Slow and steady. That was good.

"No. Mitzi the alligator. She lives in the pond across the compound, Normally, she stays far away from humans. I'm not sure why she charged, even with the storm. When did she get you?"

"Right after I got here. Snagged my thigh."

Lucy's thoughts flashed back to him crouching in the yard. That suddenly made more sense now. Her stomach dropped. "So, you've been running around here this whole time with a huge gash in your thigh?"

"Wasn't that bad." He opened his other eye and shifted slightly, wincing. "Superficial cut. Or at least it was, until the corner of the metal shutter caught it."

"Oh God," she gasped. "It's a miracle you made it back to the porch."

"The miracle is I got the window covered. You better secure that before the wind blows it in."

Lucy spun to see the back door shuddering

on its hinges, even with the dead bolt in place and the screened-in porch as an added barrier.

She grabbed the lantern and hurried to her office, where she'd stashed the metal bars to bracket it in one of her desk drawers. Anxious bile scalded her throat, but there'd be plenty of time for that later. She grabbed the bars then rushed back to the kitchen to shove them into place. There. Secure. She took a deep breath and leaned back against the wood. The house was as protected as it was going to get.

Which left Jackson.

He shifted so his wounded leg faced the chair opposite him and started to lift it.

"No, don't!" She moved quickly to his side. "You could make the bleeding worse."

"I'm a paramedic. I know what I'm doing." He clenched his jaw and reached for his calf, batting her hands away when she tried to help, and pulled his leg up on the chair, hissing between clenched teeth.

"And you call me stubborn," she said, scowling as she moved a third chair under his foot so the whole leg was supported. Lucy pulled the lantern closer so she could see. "Sit back."

"It's not that bad," he said, pulling at the torn fabric of his pants to inspect the wound himself. "The metal sheet jolted it, that's all. I'll be fine. Got some thread and a needle?"

"What?" She gave him an incredulous stare. "You going to suture yourself, too?"

"Maybe."

Exasperated, she threw her hands in the air. "Don't be stupid. I'm a veterinarian. I stitch up my animal patients all the time. I'm probably better at it and faster than you. And I'll be neater, too, since I can actually see what I'm doing." Grumbling, Lucy headed down to the basement for the supplies she'd stowed there earlier, taking a second to soothe her animals, then hurried back to the kitchen.

After scrubbing her hands with soap and rinsing with bottled water over the empty side of her double sink, she pulled on surgical gloves, then laid a sterile cloth on the table and quickly organized her supplies so she could reach them. "I'll need you to hold the lantern so I can see. If you feel the least bit woozy, tell me and I'll stop. Warn me if you have to move."

She knelt beside him and plucked at the ragged edges of his torn pants. The tear in the fabric was about five inches long, but she was relieved to find after peeling the fabric away that the wound was shorter by about two inches. Still, it looked deep and definitely needed cleaning. And stitching.

Lucy reached for the scissors to widen the hole in his pants, but he beat her to them.

"Tell me what you want and I'll hand it to you," he said, giving her a look.

"I *want* you to follow directions."

He snorted. "You're one to talk."

The last thing Lucy should want to do at that moment was smile. She absolutely should *not* enjoy their verbal sparring. Except she kind of did. She avoided Jackson's gaze as she deftly slit the fabric, elongating the tear.

"Be careful. This is my work uniform, you know."

"Get a new one. I have to clean this wound properly or it could get infected." She hazarded a glance up at him, then returned to her task, unable to stop her slight grin now. "And that's Dr. Lucy to you."

Jackson smiled in return. "Luis couldn't stop gushing about your program with the therapy pets when I asked him. He thinks very highly of you."

He asked his brother about me?

She focused more than was necessary on the task at hand, squashing those odd butterflies swarming inside her at his words. Lucy cleansed the wound with antiseptic, then reached for a syringe packet and vial of anesthetic and drew up the medication.

"I don't need a shot," Jackson said, his tone tense. "Don't like needles, at least when they're directed at me."

"Close your eyes. It will only sting a little." She placed a gloved hand on his muscled thigh to steady it as she gave the injection.

"Ouch! Dammit, that— Ouch!" He swore under his breath. "I think you gave me enough for a small elephant."

"I gave you the correct dose for an adult male." She set the used syringe aside and picked up the suture packet next, waiting for the meds to take effect. "Won't be long now."

He stayed silent, staring at the far wall

while she tapped the skin around his wound to make sure it was numb. The wound was small enough, thankfully, and she soon began. Tying off the first stitch and snipping it with a pair of surgical scissors, she then went in for the second. From the length of the laceration, she was thinking five should do it. "All right?"

"Fine," he murmured, still not looking down. "I've been through worse."

Lucy continued working, making small talk to distract herself and him. "Really? How?"

"Coast guard. Four years." His expression tightened. "Why'd you become a vet?"

She shrugged slightly then moved on to the third stitch. "It's my calling. I've always loved animals. I volunteered at a shelter and met Dr. Dave. He helped me get into the vet program at Clemson University before he and his partner moved to the Keys. When I decided to set up a practice of my own, Dr. Dave recommended Big Pine Key, and the rest is history."

"Is your family in South Carolina still?"

"Charleston." Lucy tried not to tense at his digging into her past and failed. The hurt of

Robert's betrayal and her parents' complicity was still too fresh, too raw. She kept working. "Just a few more sutures and we're done."

Jackson took a deep breath. "How'd you end up with the gator?"

"She came with the property. Been here for a few years, according to Dr. Dave. She minds her own business and hunts away from here, returning to her nest each night. And she beats a normal security system any day of the week."

"Got that right." He shook his head, meeting her gaze at last, his smile wry. "You surprise me at every turn, Lucy."

"Same," she said, the moment drawing out between them, shimmering with possibilities.

A strange bubble of awareness swelled inside her like a balloon, filling her up, pushing all her doubts and fears aside until the wind sent something else crashing into the side of the house. Jackson flinched and looked away. Lucy steadied the needle and tied off the last knot, then bandaged his wound. Working in difficult situations was crucial in her profession, even with the adrenaline fizzing through her system.

Good thing, too, since Mathilda and the man sitting before her had officially blown her quiet, peaceful life to hell.

Finally finished, she stood to clean up the mess. Jackson watched her, her skin tingling in the wake of his perusal. It was unsettling, and she focused on wrapping up the small pile she'd made in the sterile cloth, not him. "The numbness will wear off soon. You should take some pain meds. They're in the box."

"Thanks." He found the acetaminophen, and Lucy got him a bottled water from the cooler in the basement. She did her best not to notice the sleek muscles of his throat working as he swallowed and inspected the bandaged area around his wound instead. Assured it was good, Lucy helped him lower his foot to the floor. Despite the lidocaine, he winced.

"Need to stand," Jackson said. Using her shoulders for leverage, he got himself upright, then paused.

"Okay?" she asked.

"Perfect." He reached toward her, and for a crazy moment, Lucy thought he might cup her cheek. She moved back, not liking to be touched unless it was her choice.

But he didn't touch her, just reached behind for a battery pack.

Good. Fine. She didn't want Jackson's hands on her.

Do I?

No. She ignored the odd stab of disappointment inside her.

Their conversation lulled once more, and the howl of the wind rushed to fill the void. She finished packing the last few boxes on the counter, relieved to find he'd moved away to sit at the table again, foot propped up and his face taut as he stared down at his hands in his lap.

The glow of the lantern only highlighted how handsome he was. Not like a movie star or Robert. Jackson had a quieter sort of sexiness. One that sneaked up on you but was all the stronger for it. Not that she noticed or cared. Nope.

She turned away from the unwanted, unexpected need throbbing in her system that had as much to do with the storm as the man trapped in the house with her.

And that terrified Lucy way more than any hurricane.

CHAPTER SEVEN

"IF YOU'RE HUNGRY, we should eat before we go to the basement. Might be a while before we have a chance again." Another loud crack resounded, and she turned instinctively toward the front windows in the living room, but with the shutters in place, she couldn't see anything outside.

Frustrated, she went into the pantry and set one of the lanterns on a shelf then scanned what was left in there to put together a quick meal. A sudden chill went through her, making her cross her arms and rub them. It was more in reaction to the turmoil surrounding the house than the temperature. She hadn't thought the cacophony could get any louder, but now the whole place seemed to vibrate from the noise alone. Maybe it was just as well she couldn't see outside.

Back in Charleston, the storms she'd been

through had never been this bad. Of course, they'd had a nice two-story in the suburbs, with a big yard and a swing set in the back, far from the coastline, so maybe that made a difference. Initially she hadn't minded being an only child, but then her issues, which had gone undiagnosed for years, had surfaced. Her parents had thought she was just quiet, an introvert. But as she'd gotten older and it was time to start school, they'd realized her problems went deeper. Her grades had been fine, outstanding even, but her tics had kept her from excelling socially. Around the age of nine, they'd taken her out of public school and put her with a private tutor because of the bullying. Lucy had tried to pretend it didn't matter, but that wasn't true. Living in a bubble wasn't any kind of life at all.

Then she'd met Robert through her tutor. He'd been bullied too as a kid—not because of any issues, but because he was so smart. He'd graduated high school at fifteen and gone on to college early to study psychology. He found Lucy fascinating, and they'd spend hours just talking or doing puzzles or whatever. For a girl who'd been isolated her whole life, having a friend—or even better, a man interested and attracted to her—was like a miracle. She'd fallen hard and fast for him, wanting to spend every waking minute with him, and her parents had been overjoyed. Their daughter had finally found a mate.

By the time Lucy had finished high school, Robert was nearing the end of his bachelor's degree in psychology and was ready to enter a graduate program of study, specializing in anxiety disorders. He said it would bring him and Lucy even closer together, help him understand her even more. Help him help her. But in the end it had only torn them apart.

Because the more Robert tried to understand her, the more she started to feel like she was nothing but a lab experiment to him. He'd become more controlling, more manipulative, and she'd yearned for freedom. From him, from her parents, from all the constraints her issues brought down on her.

Her one bright spot had been volunteering at the local animal shelter.

That was where she'd first met Dr. Dave.

He'd become her friend, too, but a different kind of friend than she'd had before. He never tried to "help" her, never tried to control her, never used her issues against her. He just was there for her when she needed him and listened to her when she needed to talk. When he'd mentioned she might consider a career as a vet, she'd jumped at the chance. She'd graduated with top grades in her studies and had been offered multiple scholarships at colleges in the Charleston area with the letter of recommendation Dr. Dave had written her, but she'd shocked her parents and Robert by accepting one at Clemson University in Columbia, hours away from Charleston.

She'd ended her engagement with Robert and moved out of her parents' house and never looked back. After she'd finished veterinary school she'd bought this compound, on Dr. Dave's recommendation, and forged a new life for herself.

She never wanted to be trapped again. Never wanted to be controlled and manipulated.

Never wanted to become reliant on anyone else's help, because that led to disaster.

Lucy had learned that lesson well and had no intention of repeating it ever again. That's why she'd fought so hard to stay here, why she'd fought so hard against Jackson and his damned orders and interventions.

Until today. Today the storm and fate had taken that choice away from her.

But this place was her home. A part of her. She wouldn't leave. Couldn't.

She just prayed they'd survive another twenty-four hours.

A chair scraped on the floor and jarred her out of her thoughts. Right. Dinner. She headed out of the pantry, back into the kitchen. Open and airy, it was her favorite room in the house, aside from the clinic, where she spent the most time. Jackson's back was to her, his head bent as he examined his wound. Her fingertips buzzed, remembering the feel of his warm, smooth skin, the muscles firm as marble beneath. She'd done a good job. He shouldn't even have a scar when it healed fully.

Her gaze drifted over his torso and down

the length of his leg propped on her kitchen chair. Another unwanted frisson of awareness raced up her spine. She really didn't know much about him, other than he was a paramedic and adopted. She imagined him running into a crisis, saving kids and puppies and old people.

"I don't mind you checking me out, but maybe we should get a move on before Mathilda arrives."

Oh God. Busted.

Mortified heat spread from her core to her extremities, worse even than when she'd been bullied. She felt guilty and exposed and more than a little dazed and confused.

Lucy went back in the pantry, ears burning and hands shaking. The voice in her head was right. She could do this. She was in control. She'd worked way too hard for her peace of mind to let him jeopardize it now. Besides, she had no business being attracted to him. From what she had seen of Jackson so far, he was a total control freak who seemed to think he needed to rescue everyone in sight, which meant he was just like Robert. He'd only cared about her because he'd wanted to take care of her, too.

But Lucy didn't need to be taken care of. She could take care of herself.

After a deep breath to calm her nerves, she studied the shelves again. She'd already packed up most of the contents of her refrigerator in the cooler downstairs, so tortilla chips and a can of nacho dip looked like the best choice. She stood on an overturned bucket to reach the top shelf, but just as her hand closed around the can, the stupid bucket shifted and she lost her balance, nearly toppling to the floor in a painful heap—if not for the strong arms that closed around her from behind.

"What the hell are you doing now?" Jackson asked. His deep voice, rife with annoyance, rumbled through the solid chest pressed to her back.

"Getting food." She struggled against his hold. The last thing she needed was him thinking she was a klutz on top of the rest of her issues. Of course, the fact she still cared at all what he thought did little to improve her mood. She finally pulled away then gave him an irritated stare. "I told you to stay put."

His strong hands still braced her upper arms, and her skin tingled from his touch. He stood close enough she could see the hint of dark stubble on his jaw. "You sure you're okay?"

"Great." She swallowed hard, wondering when exactly it had gotten so hot in there.

He watched her a moment, frowning. "Lucy?"

She concentrated on the shelf behind him as her OCD spiked and her tics took over. There were five boxes of corn bread mix, but there should've been six. Why weren't there six? She always bought them in even numbers and made sure to stock up often, so they stayed even. Now they were odd. She stepped past him and began to fiddle with the boxes, searching behind and around them for the missing box. The storm outside had nothing on the whirling tornado of anxiety inside her. She was getting lost again, lost in the weeds of her disorder...

Then his fingertip nudged her chin upward,

and she met his eyes. Her pulse stuttered, but she couldn't look away, trapped like a deer in headlights.

Jackson narrowed his gaze, watching her more intently as he reached over and turned down the lantern, plunging the small space into shadows.

Her heart slammed harder against her rib cage, an odd mix of apprehension and anticipation crashing over her like a tsunami. "Wh—what are you doing?"

Time screeched to a halt as he pulled her against his chest, one arm around her waist, the other around her upper back, his hand in her hair, cupping the nape of her neck as he pressed her cheek against his shoulder. She stood completely still, too stunned to react, to move away, to do anything but let him hold her.

"Put your arms around me," Jackson whispered against her scalp.

Like a robot, she looped them around his lean waist.

"Tighter."

She squeezed, feeling his hard body press

into her soft curves. Like a life preserver in a riptide, she found herself hanging on for dear life, yet battling it every step of the way. She couldn't let him in, couldn't let him close, because if she did, she'd lose everything she'd gained. "Jackson?"

"Hmm?" His voice hummed beneath her ear.

"Let me go."

He stiffened, then released her before turning the lantern back up and moving away. She missed the heat of him immediately, crossing her arms as he hobbled back to his seat at the table. He flopped down, looking about as discombobulated as she felt. Finally, he said, "Sorry."

Me too. She left the pantry and opened the can of dip at the counter, grabbing a spoon from the drawer without looking before carrying it all over to the table, along with the chips. Taking a seat across from him she handed him a plate. "I'm sorry you came here."

"Don't be," he said, his tone defeated. "It was my choice."

She frowned. "I still don't understand why."

"You need help, and I came to provide it. That's what EMTs are supposed to do, right?" He shrugged. "Anyway, it doesn't matter now. We're stuck and need to make the best of it until the storm blows over."

"Yes." She reached for the dip at the same moment he did, their fingers tangling. She pulled away fast and mumbled, "Sorry…"

"You need to stop saying that." He winked at her then started to get up again. "Got any napkins?"

"I'll get them," she said, also rising.

"I'm not an invalid." He hobbled across the room.

She watched him go, unable to forget their brief hug. Which was stupid, because she didn't want his hugs. Didn't want him touching her and holding her and caring about her.

Do I?

They ate the rest of the food in silence.

Finally, she tucked her hair behind her ear, toying with her empty soda can. "Hope you had enough."

"Yep. It was good. Thanks." He held her

gaze a moment then pulled out his phone. "Got any reception?"

She pulled out her own device and checked the bars. "Nope."

Boom! Screech!

They both stared at the ceiling as the storm intensified once more.

Wide-eyed, Lucy stared at him. "What do you think that was?"

"Roof damage, I'm guessing," Jackson said, cursing under his breath. "Don't think it's major, though, otherwise the sound would've gotten louder."

Lucy was already in the hallway heading for the stairs to the second floor. "I'm going to take a look."

"No." Jackson's chair scraped on the hardwood. "Lucy, stop!"

Her steps faltered, and she looked back at him. "You said it was probably nothing major."

"No. I said I thought the roof was still on, not that it wasn't serious." He followed her down the hall, using a mop handle from the pantry like a crutch. "We should go to the basement now."

Her mind raced, and her palms dampened. A panic attack loomed dead ahead unless she got it under control. Lucy took a deep breath and closed her eyes.

You can do this. You're in control.

Then Jackson was at her side, distracting her. "I didn't see anything comfortable to sit on when I was down there earlier. Can we take the couch cushions down with us?"

"Yes."

"Good, I'll get them."

He squeezed past her, stopping far too close for her comfort to look down at her. "Is there a bedroom on this floor?"

"What?" Her mind was still a chaotic mess of panic. She couldn't think, couldn't speak, couldn't…

"A bedroom, Lucy," he repeated, sterner this time. "Is there one down here?"

"Yes. Why?" She licked her dry lips and Jackson's gaze tracked that tiny movement, his eyes darkening. Lucy scrambled to find balance again. "I'll, uh, get the sofa cushions."

"I'll get the cushions." Jackson didn't move out of her way. "Single or double?"

She couldn't process his question. Couldn't make sense of anything but the heat of him surrounding her, making her want things she had no business wanting. All she knew was if she tried to get past him, she'd press up against him way more intimately than she'd been during their hug earlier, and that set off a whole new bunch of alarms in her head.

"Lucy," he repeated, his brusque tone slicing through the chaos inside her. "Is the bed down here single or double?"

"Queen."

"Good. Go start taking off the sheets. I'll be in to help you in a minute."

Jackson finally moved away so she could get past him, and it took most of Lucy's willpower not to break into a run. She swore she could still feel him behind her. She should be concerned about the hurricane outside, not the wild effect of Jackson on her equilibrium.

CHAPTER EIGHT

JACKSON LEANED AGAINST the wall, as much to watch her walk away as to rest his aching leg.

Once he'd tossed the sofa cushions down the stairs, he went to the bedroom to check on Lucy and stopped dead on the threshold.

The sight of her kneeling on all fours to yank the far corner of the fitted sheet off the bed shouldn't have affected him the way it did, but damn if his pulse didn't trip, and heat rose from beneath the collar of his shirt to claw up his neck. He cleared his throat and hopped into the room to grab the opposite corner.

"Let me help," he said, freeing one corner at the same moment she gave a mighty tug on the opposite side, sending her sprawling back into the center of the bed with the sheets tangled between her legs.

Well, hell.

Lucy caught him staring and gave him a dour look, then wadded up the sheet and tossed it to the floor before scrambling off the bed.

Just as well.

He sighed and bent to heave the mattress to one side. With luck, the worst of the storm would be over tomorrow and he could get back to Key West and resume his IC role. So far, cell service was still out. With luck, when it came time to explain why he had handed over command to Luis temporarily, the review board would give him a chance to defend his need to come to Big Pine Key and take into consideration his efforts to save an innocent life.

Jackson looked up again to find Lucy across from him now, her position giving him a clear view straight down the front of her white tank top. Exactly what he didn't need. He swallowed hard and glanced away fast—but not before he caught her arched brow and defiant expression.

Busted.

Dammit. He would not look again. Would

not. Except his eyes drifted back to her chest, as if of their own volition. Off-kilter, in more ways than one, Jackson concentrated on moving the heavy mattress, perspiration glistening on his forehead. He felt a little woozy, too, and his pulse was erratic. Maybe he had lost more blood than he'd thought. He should probably rest, but they needed to get this thing down to the basement first.

He took a good hold on the mattress and gave a vicious tug, grunting and pulling the thing half off the bed so fast he barely had time to hop out of the way to keep it from falling on him. Once they'd maneuvered it out into the living room, Jackson motioned to Lucy to change ends with him. "You push, I'll pull."

"Explain to me why we're doing this?"

"To cover our heads and the cages. If the roof caves in, then we'll have a passing chance of not getting crushed."

"Isn't that what basements are for?" She sounded as exasperated as he felt.

Jackson dropped his forehead in the soft bedding and prayed for patience. "Yes, but this house is old, and I don't trust the structure. If the top floor goes, the whole thing could cave right in on us." He angled his head to one side so he could see her. "Okay? Good. Now push."

Lucy ducked back behind her end and together they maneuvered the heavy, bulky thing downstairs.

"I'm going to move this out of the way and you stack some of those supply boxes in the middle of the space here," Jackson said, pointing to the center of where the mattress sat on the floor. "Then we'll set a cage at each corner for support."

Now that she understood his plan, Lucy worked efficiently, arranging things on her side while Jackson did the same on his. He seemed to be moving around fine with his wound and makeshift crutch, which was good. She'd expected it to give him more trouble. And speaking of trouble, after their encounter in the pantry and again in the hall, she now couldn't seem to stop noticing him as a man, instead of just a warm body she was stuck with during the storm. Each time she looked over at Jackson, all she could see was his muscled shoulders and flexing biceps as he shoved things around, or how his taut butt looked in those black pants when he bent over. It was frustrating as hell, especially with anxiety still buzzing beneath her surface.

With a sigh, she moved King's cage into place, careful to not jar his IV bag, then stopped to waggle a playful finger at him through the bars. He remained sound asleep, though, and she stood and wiped her hands on her jeans. "What next?"

"We bring down the last of those boxes from the kitchen, then secure ourselves in for the night."

They were done in under ten minutes. Lucy stowed the lanterns and flashlights where she could reach them. Jackson shoved the cooler she'd filled earlier off to one side then went back up to bar the door at the top of the stairs. Once everything was in its place, she turned in a slow circle and surveyed the basement.

The animals were oddly quiet, either sleeping or spooked.

"Right," Jackson huffed out, the mattress leaning on his shoulder. "Let's get this over our heads."

She grabbed one side, and together they propped the thing partially up onto the top of the cages. The animals were awake now, that was for sure. A chorus of meows and squawks and barks from Sam filled the air, drowning out the noise from outside. Sam kept getting underfoot, nearly tripping her, and suddenly Jackson's face was far too close to her chest for comfort.

"If it were up to me," he said into her shirt, his hot breath causing goose bumps to break out on her skin. "I'd spend the next several hours right here. But if we're going to get this done, you need to move back."

Crap.

You can do this. You're in control.

Lucy let go of the mattress and stumbled backward.

The thing slipped, its trajectory putting him on a collision course with her once again.

One instant Jackson was on his side of the space. The next she was flat against the wall, his body pressing into hers. For a moment, Lucy didn't dare move, didn't dare breathe, not with the shoulder-to-belly-to-toe contact. All that power, all those muscles, all of his barely restrained…

Then he pushed back onto one elbow to look at her, and she closed eyes to hide her shame.

You can do this. You're in control.

Except she didn't feel in control, and she had serious doubts whether she could do this at all. Part of her wanted to stay right where she was forever. The other part of her wanted to run from the house and take her chances with the hurricane. Neither was an option. Not with his body holding hers in place, his warmth, his scent, his masculine presence surrounding her.

"All right?" he asked, his breath stirring the hair near her temple.

"Great," Lucy whispered past her tight throat with all the sarcasm she could muster. "You?"

"Same."

His gentle joke helped lift some of her inner tension and she relaxed a tad, staring past his shoulder. A strange intimacy crackled between them now, one that had a question popping out of her mouth before she could stop it. "Why did you hug me?"

When Jackson didn't answer, she hazarded a glance at his face, only to find him watching her.

Summoning all her courage, she kept her gaze on his, nose to nose, and persisted. "Earlier, in the pantry. Why did you turn off the lantern and hug me?"

In response, he lifted his weight from her, and she scrambled away, taking care not to bang against him as they moved the mattress into place. Her OCD wanted her to tic again, to straighten all the cages, check the knob on the basement door, walk the perimeter of the basement and count her steps, divide the number by three and hope it came out even…

"Here," Jackson said, tossing her a couch cushion.

It thumped softly against her chest, knocking her out of her anxious spiral. She took a deep breath, feeling some of the pressure inside her ease. Funny how he could do that, calm her down like that. No one had been able to do that since...

Nope. Not going there.

You can do this. You're in control.

"Thanks," she said, crawling inside their makeshift fort then arranging two cushions on her side of the space before settling down, cross legged. The cages were high enough with the boxes stacked in the middle that they could sit up straight, not hunkered over. Jackson took a seat across from her and stretched his legs out, grimacing.

Concerned, she asked, "How's your leg?"

"I'll live."

"Maybe I should take another look. Move the lantern this way a few inches." She motioned with one hand but didn't look up. He didn't reply, but the light shifted. Lucy moved the torn fabric of his pants away and peeled back part of the bandage. "It's red and there's some more bleeding, but none of the stitches popped."

"You do right good work," he said, his voice low.

"Thanks." Lucy looked up then regretted it as her simmering attraction to him notched higher toward full boil. Voice gruff, she coughed to clear her throat. "Let me get you another dose of pain meds."

She started to scoot away, but Jackson stopped her, his hand on her arm.

"Relax. I know you're worried, but don't add me to your list of things to be concerned about, okay? Maybe check on your other patients."

She looked around at King, Sam and Bubba. The kitten was asleep again, Sam was settling into his bed and Bubba was chewing on his toy.

Jackson rubbed her forearm, then his touch dropped away. "You don't like people caring about you. Why?"

He hadn't answered her questions before about the hug—no reason for her to do any differently. She didn't want him or anyone else poking into her business, taking over, thinking they knew best, no matter how well-intentioned.

Lucy slumped back onto her side of the cushions and said after a long moment, "I like being self-sufficient. Why do you like being in control?"

"Because I'm the one others depend on. I'm the hero. That's my value." Restlessness sparkled in his gaze as he turned the spotlight back on her. "There's a difference between self-sufficiency and just plain stubbornness and self-sabotage."

"And how would you know?" she said, scooting farther back until her back hit the side of Bubba's cage. The bird reached through the bars to grab a length of her hair in its beak, cleaning it. "You know what? Forget I asked."

"What if I don't want to?" Jackson countered, ignoring the imaginary Keep Out sign above her head. He wasn't comfortable with this conversation, either—or the woman he was having it with—yet he couldn't seem to let the matter drop. "Why won't you accept help, Lucy? Why won't you let anyone in?"

Why won't you let me in?

Her expression grew remote again, and he winced. Dammit. He shouldn't care. He was used to distancing himself from those he treated in order to do his job, kept his professional walls up in case things didn't go to plan. Otherwise, he couldn't live with the loss. And yes, maybe those defensive mechanisms extended to his personal life as well, but after being abandoned by his birth mother, it was amazing he'd learned to cope at all.

"Let's make a deal. If you tell me why you hugged me, then I'll tell you why I don't like to accept help and why this place is so important to me," she said, turning to give Bubba a kiss.

Jackson felt oddly jealous of that silly bird. Maybe that's why he answered, "I hugged you because I thought you needed one."

She froze, then looked back at him, her

gaze dubious. "You don't strike me as a guy in touch with his emotions."

He shrugged. "Emotion had nothing to do with it."

"Pretty sure emotion has everything to do with it." Thrust into a minefield, going forward felt safer than retracing her steps. "Hugging is all about connection and feelings. That's why people do it."

His expression darkened, and he arched a brow. "Not me. No connections. That's my rule."

The excess energy bubbling through her system felt like champagne shaken to the point of exploding. She flexed her fingers to relieve some of it. At least the urge to tic had lessened. And whatever was going on between them, she wasn't about to let him get the upper hand. "Know what I think?"

"If I lie and say yes will you spare me?"

"I think you hugged me because you needed one, too."

Jackson scoffed. "Whatever."

Sensing she'd hit a bull's-eye, Lucy pressed

on. "What I can't figure out is why you turned out the light. Maybe the darkness is like a mental cloak? You don't have to think, just act. Give in to instinct."

"Really?" He scowled and shifted his weight, his words emerging more as a rough purr, dangerous as a panther ready to pounce. "And what do you know about instincts, Lucy? When do you give in to yours?"

The temperature in the basement seemed to rise several degrees in the span of a second, but she refused to be deterred. "I try not to give in to instincts at all."

Jackson's lips compressed. "Then that's where we differ."

A tingle zinged through her core, and her pulse sped. "Because your instincts guide you?"

"I live by mine, but that's not what I meant."

"What did you mean, then?" That had come out far breathier than she'd wanted.

You can do this. You're in control.

"Because I think we both rely on instinct to save us. Only I don't lie to myself about it." He leaned forward, leaving only inches between them, and her breath caught. Time slowed as he ran a fingertip down the length of her nose, letting it rest on her bottom lip. "The real question is, Lucy, what do you think will happen if you let someone in, let them help you?"

The unexpected caress had her nerve endings going haywire, and she answered without thinking. "I'll get trapped again. Used. Manipulated."

He frowned. "Is that what happened before?"

"No." *Yes.* She pulled away and scooted back to her side of the small space to rummage through the cooler for a water. As she held the cool plastic to her hot cheeks, the irony smacked her right between the eyes. She might well survive the storm, only to fall prey to her own foolish reaction to Jackson.

He pulled out his phone again. "Maybe we can find out what's going on outside."

Glad to have something to think about besides him, she drank her water and waited. She'd rather listen to damage reports and the very real possibility her home might be destroyed rather than sit in this small shadowed space with Jackson and dredge up painful memories best left buried.

"Two bars," he said triumphantly, turning his phone speaker on and raising the volume so the announcer's voice echoed off the concrete basement walls.

"...heading toward Cuba, picking up speed over the open water. Mathilda's outer bands are expected to skirt right over the Keys around three tomorrow morning—just a few hours from now—and the entire area is on high alert. No matter where you are in this storm's path, there is imminent potential for loss of life, and damage to property has been estimated to reach well into the billions."

The phone went dead, and Lucy looked from it to Jackson.

"It'll be okay," he said. "We'll make it."

In the next instant, a tremendous crash reverberated through the house with enough force to rattle the cages and send the animals into a frenzy. Bubba squawked "Welcome to the Jungle" over and over. Sam curled into a quivering bundle beside Lucy's thigh, and

Jackson did his best to comfort poor King. Somehow, she and Jackson had ended up side by side, too, with one of his arms around her shoulders and the other placed protectively over King's cage.

Resting on his good hip, he tucked her closer to his side, his wounded leg brushing hers. He looked down at her, then squeezed her closer.

"I think we're okay," she said.

"Me too." His hand felt strong and reassuring on her shoulder. It wasn't until he ran his fingers through her hair that she realized he was trembling, too.

"Know what I could use?" he whispered, so softly she would've missed it if she hadn't been paying attention.

"Hmm?" Her gaze held steady on his.

"I think I could use another hug."

She froze but didn't withdraw as he removed his arm from atop King's cage to lower the lantern light. Shadows surrounded them as Jackson gathered Lucy close once more and held her firm against his chest. Then, as if that wasn't close enough, he tucked her head under his chin.

Only then, in the darkness, did she feel safe letting her guard down, just a little. Maybe there was something to her theory after all. As the storm raged outside, tearing apart everything she'd worked so hard to build for the last year or so, Lucy buried her face against the base of his neck and inhaled deep, smelling soap and sweat and something uniquely Jackson. And with his heart pounding strong and steady beneath her ear, Lucy slipped her hands around his waist and hugged him back, making a final, desperate grab for the rapidly crumbling barriers around her heart. "Just so we're clear, I'm helping you out here. Not the other way around."

His arms tightened around her, and she felt him smile. "Duly noted."

CHAPTER NINE

JACKSON SAT THERE in the dark, holding Lucy, the noise of the storm raging overhead. But it was the feel of her hands at the small of his back that finally broke him. He'd tried hard to shut out the voices in his head, the ones telling him to keep his walls up, to not let anyone in, to avoid being vulnerable at any cost. The same voices he'd listened to since he'd been four years old and watched his mother drive away, never to return again.

He'd kept those barriers high and strong for two decades.

Until tonight.

Seemed all it took to crumble them down was one quiet, quirky woman with a spirit of steel and a soft spot for wounded creatures.

She'd spoken the truth earlier, about the darkness. He had acted on instinct both times he'd shut off the light—only now his motivation wasn't as simple as a hug. Nope. This time his needs were deeper, riskier. This time he wanted intimacy. Not just sex, but something more powerful. It clawed at him, leaving him raw inside, grasping for whatever was available as a defense and bringing him up short.

The very last thing he wanted—ever, ever again—was to *need* someone, to truly care for them.

And yes, he cared for his parents, for Luis, for his patients.

But this was different.

With Lucy, he wanted to keep her safe. He wanted to hold her and kiss her and swear that no one else would ever hurt her again. God. She was the last person he should be attracted to, and yet she'd brought him a sense of solace he'd never expected to feel again.

He didn't want to want her, and yet he did. He wanted so badly he burned.

"Lucy?" The word came out rougher than he'd intended.

"What?" She started to pull away, put some

space between them, but he wasn't ready and tightened his arms around her, keeping her in place.

"Tell me more about Mitzi," he asked, hoping to distract them both. "From what I know, alligators are social creatures, so why does she stay here with you?"

She relaxed against him once more, her breasts brushing his chest, and Jackson struggled to steady his pulse beating under her cheek. "I'm not sure. Normally, they do spend their time with their own kind."

"What makes her different, then?" *What makes me different?*

"Her rear left leg was almost completely severed in a steel trap designed to catch small mammals. The original owners brought her to this compound because it was the closest area with a private pond. It was either bring her here or leave her to die."

"Wait. The gator that attacked me only has three legs?" He sighed. "Doesn't do much for my ego."

"Don't feel bad." Lucy laughed. "Mitzi still

moves pretty darn fast, though usually it's in the other direction when humans are involved. Alligators generally prefer smaller, easily captured meals. They're cold-blooded and notorious for not expending any unnecessary energy."

"I wonder why she attacked me, then?" He frowned.

Lucy shrugged. "She's a very protective mother-to-be. The winds and impending storm probably confused her and you had the misfortune of coming between her and her nest. And you did ignore the signs, too."

"What signs?"

"The ones by the front gate. You didn't see them before when you brought King here?"

"No. I came in the back way. Plus, I was distracted because of his injuries, so…" The kitten meowed, as if realizing they were talking about him, and Jackson cooed to the little guy. "There's my brave boy. Yes, sir. Such a brave boy."

"I'm sorry you didn't know about Mitzi earlier." Lucy snuggled closer, tucking her head beneath his chin. "Most of the people on the island who visit my clinic know about her, so I guess I didn't think about it."

"It's okay." He frowned into the darkness, rubbing her back absently. "But I hope you didn't stay on her account. I'm pretty sure the rest of the wild gators in Florida ride out hurricanes on their own, nests or not. Chances are Mitzi would've been fine."

"Maybe." Lucy sighed and guilt pinched his chest. Who was he to judge someone else's choices when it came to love and devotion? Especially when his own track record there was less than stellar. He shifted on his cushion, uncomfortable in more ways than one.

"But…" Her arms tightened around him, and it took what was left of his control not to bend down and kiss her.

"Tell me," he coaxed.

She started to pull away again, but he held her tighter and whispered against her temple, "Darkness is a cloak, remember? Shut your eyes and let the words out, Lucy. Tell me why you'd willingly do something so self-destructive." His mouth grazed her skin, and he swallowed a groan. "Tell me."

* * *

"I…uh…"

Never in a million years had Lucy expected to have this conversation with him, but here she was, and if his firm embrace was any indication, she wasn't going anywhere anytime soon.

She took a deep breath and stared blankly in front of her, losing herself in the shadows. "This compound is my safe spot, my sanctuary, as much as it is for the animals I treat. No one controls me here. No one tries to use my own feelings and issues against me. I stayed here because this is where I belong, where I'm safe. When I'm here there's no games, no hidden agendas, no regrets."

Blood pounded in her ears as the silence stretched between them. She'd never told anyone the truth about what had happened with Robert. How, in the end, she'd been nothing but an experiment to him, a means to the end he wanted. A glorified lab rat. It was humiliating. It was dehumanizing. It was heartbreaking.

Yet as she sat there with Jackson, his strength

braced behind her, she wanted to tell him everything. He made her feel safe. Truly safe. Safe enough to speak her truth without fear that her words would be twisted around and used against her. Safe enough to let him help her without worrying that it made her weak.

Safe enough to connect.

Ever since Robert had betrayed her trust and her parents had been complicit in his actions, she'd successfully shut off her emotions, unwilling and unable to risk her heart. The only time she let her guard down was with her animals. She'd never once regretted her self-imposed isolation.

Until now.

Then Jackson had tried to rescue her and refused to take no for an answer. In the past, she'd rebelled against that kind of forced control. Now, she'd surrendered to Jackson. Why? Maybe because they could both be swept away with the storm. Maybe because when she looked past his charming exterior, she glimpsed a man as emotionally scarred as her. Maybe because he'd made her feel things tonight, things she'd never expected to feel again—joy, anticipation, yearning.

Against all odds and against her better judgment.

In the end, it didn't really matter, she supposed. The fact was, their lives were on the line and her nerves were rubbed raw and she wanted to open up to him, to share all her secrets, and she wanted him to confide in her as well.

After a long pause, the floodgates broke, and her inner thoughts tumbled out in a heated rush. "I let someone in. Someone I thought I could trust, but I was wrong. Not my parents, but they were part of the problem, too. This person used me. I thought they loved me, but I was mistaken."

Jackson traced his fingertips along her arm from elbow to bicep to shoulder, then paused a second before his hand drifted back down again. "You want to tell me more?"

The question sent her over some unforeseen edge, and she shattered.

She did. She really, really did. But between

the storm and the anxiety roaring through her bloodstream like a runaway freight train, it was all too much. His voice, his arms. His hands, his body, his strength. The dark, the storm, the small room. Her pulse, her want had her turning in his arms and…

Oh God. What the hell am I doing?

Lucy wanted out. Had to get out. Away from Jackson, away from the way he made her feel, away from the things she wanted to say. Away from the things she wanted to do.

Light. Air. Blessed quiet. She desperately wanted them all, both outside and in her head. It was overwhelming, waiting for the moment when her OCD would turn all these perfect moments black, erasing the easiness she currently enjoyed with Jackson. Because her issues ruined everything. If she'd been normal, maybe things with Robert would've worked out. If she'd been normal, maybe she would've been married now, with kids and a white picket fence. If she'd been normal, maybe she wouldn't be alone on this island, with a man she'd barely known a week ago, preparing to possibly die soon.

Oh God.

Suffocating. She was suffocating. Unable to breathe, unable to connect. Unable to let him in, no matter how badly her heart cried out for her to do so.

Slowly, like he was approaching a wounded animal, Jackson soothed her, his hands running up and down her back until she calmed. "Hey. Shh... It's okay. We don't have to talk. It's none of my business."

Lucy continued taking deep breaths, willing away the panic attack looming on the edges of her mind, forcing hoarse words past her constricted vocal cords. "Distract me. Tell me something about you. What were you like growing up?"

Now it was his turn to tense. "You don't really want to hear about that."

"Please. I do. I bet you were a handful."

Silence.

"If I guess will you tell me?"

His arms loosened a bit, and his pulse slowed. Better.

She smiled, the tension squeezing her chest easing. "You don't think I can, do you?"

He shrugged. "You're free to try."

She leaned back to look up at him, even though she couldn't make out much of his face in the darkness. "Promise me, no lies."

"Never." The sincerity in his tone made her believe him.

"Okay." She settled against him once more and imagined a young Jackson. "I bet you were a leader even then, always taking care of other people. You said you were adopted, so maybe you grew up too fast. Always the responsible one."

"Hmm." The sound was strained, edged with reluctant interest. "Maybe."

"I'm right, aren't I? It's why you like control so much," she said, her confidence growing now that the spotlight was off her. "Take how you showed up here earlier, determined to make me leave. Like you'd vanquish this hurricane single-handedly if you could."

Jackson snorted. "For someone who doesn't play well with others, you have excellent intuition."

"What made you like that, Jackson?"

"Maybe I was just born this way."

"Were you?"

Another long pause. "Doesn't really matter now, does it?"

Her chest pinched for the boy he'd been and whatever had made him the man he was today. "I'm sorry, Jackson."

"No need. We're both just surviving."

Except suddenly surviving didn't feel like enough for her anymore. She turned slightly, until their faces were a mere breath apart. Time seemed to slow. And then he kissed her.

Warm, firm lips covered hers, his tongue wet and hot. Not devouring, not crushing, but tasting, sampling. His mouth moved over hers slowly and thoroughly, as if trying to memorize her. Savoring her as if she were a precious treasure.

Never had Lucy been so completely seduced by a simple kiss.

Except there was nothing simple about Jackson or what he made her feel.

He moved a hand from her waist to the

nape of her neck, deepening the kiss, while the other moved down to pull her hips more tightly against him. "Stop me, Lucy," he whispered, pulling away slightly. "You won't find what you're looking for. Not with me."

"Neither will you," she panted. "But this is enough."

He tilted her head back, leaning into her so his hot breath tickled her throat. "This will never be enough."

Thunder boomed, rattling the house and shaking the foundation beneath them.

She pressed herself harder against his chest, her taut nipples grazing his warmth and making her desperate for more. "I want you, Jackson. Please."

His answer was to take her mouth again. And again. Ravaging her like Mathilda was ravaging the Keys.

Lucy gripped his shoulders, grinding against him, needing, searching, anything to take the ache away. Then his knee pushed up between her legs, and yes. Oh yes. That was what she wanted. Higher, harder. It had been so long.

Too long. She clamped her thighs together to keep him there.

He growled against her neck then bucked hard.

Confused, Lucy suddenly found herself half a foot away.

Her heart raced along with her thoughts, trying to comprehend what had just happened. Jackson's harsh breaths told her where he was even though she couldn't see him in the dark. She groped for the lantern, her hand smacking against his warm, hard chest instead.

"Stay still," he hissed.

Embarrassed heat flooded her. She never threw herself at men like that. She could blame it on the storm, on her issues, on her overwhelming reaction to being cooped up in such a small, confined place, but it wouldn't wash, no matter how desperately she wished it would.

Sudden blinding light filled the space, and she shielded her eyes from the lantern's glow and Jackson's too-perceptive gaze.

"I think—" He winced and shifted his injured leg. "I'll take that painkiller now."

Oh God. She'd gotten so wrapped up in the moment she'd forgotten about his wound.

"I'm so sorry." Lucy rummaged through the box of medical supplies nearby, wishing the ground would swallow her whole as his gaze burned a hole through the side of her.

Finally, she located the bottle and held it closer to the light to check it was the right one, careful to keep her face averted. She hated being such a coward, but she'd had good reasons for keeping her distance from people, and what had happened with Jackson just now had proved her instincts were right.

"I doubt those pills cure what ails us."

So much for avoiding the subject. Lucy sighed and held out the bottle to him, without looking, glad her hand was steady. "Take two of these while I get you some water."

But instead of the bottle, he latched on to her wrist, pulling her toward him while he used his free hand to tilt up her chin. Lucy summoned all her strength not to yank out of his grasp and scurry backward like an awkward crab. But there was nothing she could do about her trembling.

"Damn, woman. You've got this retreat thing down to a science, don't you?" he asked, gaze narrowed. "I mean, I thought I was good at getting out fast, but you've got me beat."

She opened her mouth—whether to breathe or speak, Lucy wasn't sure. Not that it mattered, since she couldn't seem to do either.

"Doesn't matter." He tugged again until she was on her hands and knees, the position putting her perilously close to his mouth again. "We've got a decision to make here, and I'm not sure either of us is thinking clearly enough to pick the right option."

She frowned, her mind whirling. "Decision?"

"About whether we're going to remember all the reasons we avoid entanglements in the first place." He leaned closer, tilting his head as if he meant to kiss her, but stopped short. "Or finish what we started a few minutes ago."

CHAPTER TEN

YESTERDAY, IF ANYONE had told Jackson his heart would override his brain, he'd have said they were crazy. Except the only crazy one here now was him. And what was even worse was he didn't care.

Not with Lucy watching him with those expressive dark eyes of hers, showing all the emotions swirling inside her, the same things he was feeling—hunger, heat, desire, doubt.

His heart rate kicked up a notch. He could've pulled her against him again and been done with it, but that wasn't how this worked. If they were going to do this, he had to be sure she wanted it as much as he did. This had to be her choice.

He just hoped she made up her mind before it killed him.

"I can't... I don't..." she said at last, pulling free to slump back against the cage behind her. The sense of loss stunned Jackson, as did the immediate urge to change her mind.

What the hell is happening to me?

In the past, he could take sex or leave it. There were always plenty of women looking for a good time with no strings attached, and when things had run their course, he moved on to the next one. But now...

He shifted back, too, putting a small but effective bit of space between them to distance himself. Mentally, anyway. His tight lower body complained, but he ignored it. Discomfort was good. The pain helped him focus.

At least, it always had in the past.

"Jackson—"

He glanced over, steeling himself against the possibility of an apology, or worse, pity. No way could he handle that. That's why he hadn't told her about his birth mother. He'd dealt with enough pity for a lifetime, and once people found out about her just leaving him behind without a word, that was the default they went to. Followed closely by morbid curiosity and wariness. So, he kept his expression aloof, relieved to see her doing the same. Or at least trying. But Lucy was just too damn easy to read.

He wondered how many times her emotions had gotten her into trouble. She'd mentioned people using her, manipulating her, controlling her. Those things made him want to punch something, namely whoever had done that to her. It made him furious to think she'd been used, hurt because her heart and issues were on display for anyone to see.

"I could use that water now," he said, his voice cold.

She grabbed another bottle from the cooler and slid it across the floor toward him. "You might not want to drink too much—"

"I know we need to conserve it."

"I wasn't thinking of that so much as…" Her voice trailed off, her cheeks pinkening.

"Oh. Right. Good point." He tossed the pills down dry instead and slid the unopened bottle back to her. "Thanks."

She returned it to the cooler then checked each of the cages and their occupants before fiddling with the box of medical supplies, arranging then rearranging them as if the fate of the universe depended on her getting them in exactly the right spot.

"Lucy."

She stilled but didn't look over at him.

"Maybe we should talk about what we might be facing in the next few hours now. Come up with plans in case...you know... things don't go smoothly."

"You mean in case we die?" She crossed her legs and shifted to face him again, blunt as usual. "I'm a vet. You're a paramedic. We're both professionals. I'm sure we can handle it."

"Yeah." He gave an unpleasant chuckle. "Funny how we can deal with life and death just fine, but not anything personal."

She shrugged then pulled a baggie of fruit out of the cooler nearby and fed an orange slice to the cockatoo through the bars of its cage. "Makes sense to me. Emotions are always harder to talk about."

That got his full attention. He didn't dare react.

"I guess they are." He fiddled with the leg of his torn pants again. "That's why I try to keep mine out of it. Not everything has to mean something, right? In fact, sometimes it's better if it doesn't, since nothing lasts forever. Better to keep things light, uncomplicated."

Jackson swallowed hard, stunned he'd said that. Admitted that.

"That's an interesting take," she said thoughtfully, giving him some serious side eye.

"Whatever." He leaned his head back and stroked King's paw through the side of his cage. "So, you're saying you've never had a fling? Just hot sex and forget the rest? No strings. All the pleasure, none of the pain? Sounds like that'd be right up your alley, a loner like you."

He did it all the time. Every time, truth be told.

Her shoulders stiffened and she gave Bubba the last slice of orange before facing Jackson again, hands clenched and knees tucked to her chest like she was trying to roll herself into a tiny ball. The ultimate defensive posture. She met his gaze directly, her stern silence making it clear she'd taken his question as a challenge. "No. I haven't."

He wanted to ask her more about that ex-fiancé of hers but never had the chance.

Another tremendous boom of thunder rocked the house, so loud it hurt his ears, followed by a more horrific tearing sound. The whole house shook as if the structure above them was being ripped in two. "Get near the middle boxes!" Jackson yelled, grabbing the edge of the mattress to anchor it above their heads, pulling the corner cages closer to the center of the space near them. Lucy did the same on her side. "Stay down, close to the floor."

The wind's screeching wail made it difficult to hear what she was saying. "Is the house collapsing?"

"Maybe." He leaned closer to her as best he could. "Part's definitely gone. The sound's louder."

Her lips brushed his earlobe, and his traitorous body leaped in response, despite the situation—or maybe because of it.

"What do you think our chances are?" Lucy yelled.

Some people would fall apart, scream, go

nuts. Not his Lucy. His already high respect for her tripled. He didn't sugarcoat reality for her. She deserved the truth. "Not good."

She stilled a second, then gathered Sam closer, scooting them both into Jackson's side so she could rest her head against his neck once again. A simple action that conveyed so much. She trusted him. And never in his life had Jackson wanted to be worthy of it more.

He kissed the top of her head and tucked her legs closer to his, the wound on his thigh the least of his concerns at that point.

"Jackson?" she said.

"Mmm?"

"Thank you."

His brows drew together, and he pulled away slightly to look down at her. "For what?"

"I know I said I could handle it, but I'm glad I'm not going through this alone. And I'm sorry you might die because of me."

Yearning ached in the center of his chest. Dammit. *She* was apologizing to *him*?

Nope. Couldn't have that.

"If I'd raised the readiness level sooner, maybe neither of us would be here. Not your fault," he said gruffly. He thought about Luis and his parents and the rest of the team back in Key West and hoped they were all faring better right now.

"I'm worried about Mitzi." The sadness in her voice pulled on his heartstrings.

"I'm sure she's all right," he said, even though he wasn't sure at all.

"She'll lose her nestlings."

"Maybe." He inhaled the sweet, clean scent of her shampoo, forcing away the terror nipping around his edges. "She can have more, right?"

"Not sure. Mitzi gets around okay on three legs, but who knows if she'll mate again."

Jackson sensed there was something more she wasn't telling him. "Was there something special about this particular nest?"

"No. Not to anyone else other than me, at least." Her slight shudder turned her words wobbly. "She's just struggled so hard to make it, and I can relate. Then she got pregnant, and I wondered if she'd live this long just so she could lay her eggs."

Jackson had never let himself think about

having a family. What if something happened and he had to leave them behind? Sure, someone wonderful like the Durands might take them in, but the scars of abandonment were deep and not easily overcome.

"I helped her," Lucy said, drawing him back to the present.

"I'm sorry?" he said, frowning.

"When alligators lay their eggs, they're completely focused on the task. Normally, I wouldn't have interfered, but she was having trouble balancing and I was afraid she'd squash them as they came out. So, I helped Mitzi prop herself up so the eggs would drop into the nest."

Jackson scowled, thinking about the danger she'd risked. "You're crazy."

"Maybe. But that's why I had to stay."

"Well, you didn't have to, but—"

"This is where I'm connected, Jackson. To Mitzi, to this place. More than any person."

He lifted her chin, staring down at her. "But what about Stacy? Dr. Dave? You have connections there, too."

"They're not the same. This place is mine.

I belong here. No one can hurt me here. This place is my freedom. I won't leave it behind. I can't."

Her tone had turned defensive again, but she didn't pull away, and he forced himself to be content with that.

For several long minutes they remained silent, the ominous sounds of Hurricane Mathilda raging around them. Then Lucy said, "Your turn."

He'd made it a habit never to talk about himself, and his need for self-defense kicked in full force. Still, he tried to sound casual. "What do you want to know?"

"Answer my question from earlier." Her tone had turned shy. "I won. You owe me."

It felt weird and wrong and wonderful all at the same time, the sudden odd urge to tell her whatever she wanted to know. Jackson was tempted, for the first time in forever, to share something of himself, to risk giving a piece of himself away. To Lucy.

Dangerous, that. And precisely why he avoided true intimacy, keeping things light. Physical. Primal. Never emotional. But she was right, he did owe her. And he was a man of his word.

"I was born in Miami. Not the rich part, but still nice. My dad died in the Gulf War before I was born, so it was just me and my mom." He shifted slightly to take weight off his injured thigh.

He'd done his best to keep to the facts and sound as clinical as possible, but he must've failed, because Lucy sniffled against him and squeezed him a bit tighter. "Oh, Jackson. I'm so sorry."

"It's okay." He shrugged, though it really wasn't okay at all. "And I'm sure it wasn't any harder than what you went through. Besides, if anyone's brave around here, it's you."

"I'm not—"

"You are, Lucy. The bravest woman I've ever known." He kissed her again, swallowing any further response she might've made, doing what he'd been wanting to do since the last time. And sure, he might've been avoiding all those confusing, conflicting emotions inside him, the deep wound that had reopened with the telling of his story, but what a way to do it. Lucy was sweet and sensual in ways he'd never experienced. He'd never wanted someone so much, ever. Being with her felt unique, so tantalizing he couldn't resist.

He took the kiss deeper, plunging his fingers into her hair before trailing them down to her shoulders. She trembled and gripped his arms, hanging on for dear life, arching against him, letting him know she wanted this as much as he did.

Body, mind, soul and spirit.

Their tongues dueled, and he conceded defeat willingly, allowing her what she sought, praying like hell he had it to give.

The storm forgotten, Jackson pulled her under him, rolling half on top of her in the small, cramped space. His hands slid from her shoulders to her waist, pulling her tighter against him, needing more contact between her softness and his hardness. He lifted himself enough to pull her shirt from the waistband of her jeans as her arms twined around his neck, urging him not to break the delicious contact, and he struggled to comply. Finally, he levered himself up on one arm and she groaned her disapproval, then sucked in a sharp breath when he pushed her shirt up.

"Please." Lucy's whisper was harsh with need.

He scooted down so his face was even with her torso and kissed her stomach. "Please what?"

"Please—" She gasped as he unclasped her bra to bare her breasts. "Yes!"

He palmed her breasts, circling her taut nipples with his thumbs. "So perfect."

"That feels so good."

Then he dipped his head and took one of the taut peaks into his mouth, stroking the other between his thumb and forefinger, and she dug her nails into his scalp. He teased against her skin, "I'm guessing this feels even better?"

She moaned and writhed. He nuzzled her again, reveling in the way she reacted. So responsive.

"Jackson." Her whisper was urgent, demanding. He understood.

"I know, sweetheart, I know." He shifted, kissing lightly along the center of her stomach, lingering over her navel, finding the whole experience of discovering her in the dark both frustrating and immensely erotic. He unsnapped her jeans and pulled on the zipper.

"Wait." She reached down, tugging at him. "Come here."

Everything in him urged him to continue, but not against her wishes. He sighed then shifted upward, not pulling her shirt down, but wishing like hell his was off so he could feel her bare breasts against his chest. Favoring his sore thigh, he pulled her to him. "What, sweetheart? Was I going too fast?"

"No." She ducked her head, resting her forehead on his shoulder.

"What then? You've never made love during a hurricane?" he joked, keeping his tone light, ignoring the fact he'd called what they'd been doing lovemaking and not sex, like usual.

"No. I haven't. But that's not why I wanted you to stop."

"Then what?"

"Because I'm not… That is, I didn't think

you..." She buried her head again, muttering against his chest. "I'm almost thirty. I'm not a virgin. You'd think I could talk about this stuff without blushing."

A new and unexpected rush of affection flooded his system. His Lucy was strong and tough, and wonderfully adorable in ways he'd never imagined. He leaned down and gave her a hard, fast kiss. Because he thought she needed the reassurance, and because he damn well wanted to. "You should've let me continue. I guarantee you'd be feeling a whole lot less stressed than you do right now."

She smacked him lightly on the shoulder and laughed. "Pretty sure of yourself, aren't you?"

In his best Southern drawl, he said, "Why yes, ma'am, I am."

She hugged him tightly, and he hugged her right back. When he'd first gotten here, he couldn't wait for the storm to be over. Now, he never wanted it to end. Because then all this would be over, and he'd have to let her go. He realized that part was going to be more difficult than he'd ever thought possible.

"Jackson?"

"Yeah?"

"Does this mean we have to stop kissing?"

His body answered with a resounding no.

"Absolutely not." He ripped off his shirt, sending buttons flying, then quickly settled his mouth back on hers. Shifting to his back, and nudging Sam farther to the side, Jackson pulled Lucy half on top of him, groaning deeply at the feel of her breasts rubbing his chest. "Damn, you feel good."

"You too," she said, smiling down at him. "You too."

CHAPTER ELEVEN

LUCY WOKE UP SLOWLY. Awareness came in waves, like layers of sand falling into place. Memories of Jackson kissing her, of her kissing Jackson, of her heart pounding and his pulse racing under her lips when she licked his neck. Their hands on each other... Then he'd slowed things down by getting her to talk, teasing her into recounting stories both funny and sad about being a vet.

At some point along the way, she'd fallen asleep.

Her eyes flew open, not because of what was happening but because of what wasn't.

The noise. It was gone.

She couldn't see a thing, but she felt a heavy weight pressing against her chest and abdomen.

"Are we dead?" she whispered.

"God, I hope not," came a raspy reply.

Jackson shifted, the bristle of his beard scraping against her bare left breast.

Before she could react, he kissed her nipple, having no problem locating it without a bit of light.

She arched under his touch, a dozen things warring for her immediate attention. It was a toss-up which would win the battle, but then he shifted his attention to her other breast and things quickly slanted toward sensation, until she shoved at his shoulders. "Jackson, stop. The storm. Listen!"

With a deep, heartfelt sigh that made her smile, he lifted his head and paused. "It's over."

"You don't think it's just the eye passing over?" she asked, straining to hear any signs the storm still raged, but there was nothing except the rustle of the animals around them.

Sam whimpered from near her feet, most likely needing to go out and potty. King issued a cranky meow, and Bubba's cage rattled as he danced back and forth on his perch, squawking, "I can see clearly now!"

"No. Not the eye," Jackson said, his voice

deep and rough with sleep. "Been too long. It's over."

"We made it?" she whispered, like Mathilda might return if she knew she'd left them behind.

"Yeah. We made it."

Lucy's thoughts instantly shifted to Mitzi, and she struggled to crawl out from under Jackson. He stopped her short, however, pinning her back down on the cushions with strong hands.

"Hold on." He slid off her. "Let me make sure the only thing on top of us is this mattress."

She pulled down her shirt while he shuffled around, trying not to think about the sudden sense of loss flooding her system. This was it. Her time with Jackson was probably over. Not that they'd done anything earth-shattering. Unless you called spending hours in the arms of the sexiest man ever important. And for her it most definitely was.

"Feels sound," he said a minute later. "I'll prop this side back up, and you feel around for the lantern."

Confused and conflicted, Lucy shoved aside her seesawing emotions and switched on the light then covered her eyes with her forearm as unnatural brightness filled the small space.

When she'd adjusted, she opened an eye and peered at Jackson, who was squinting back at her.

"I feel like a mole," he said.

"Same." She smiled, then checked on each animal and gave them each food and water before taking her own meds. "Is it day or night?"

"Uh…" Jackson glanced at his smart watch. "Morning. A bit past seven, if this thing is still right."

"Good. The sun should be up, so at least we'll be able to see the damage outside." She pulled out her phone. "Any bars yet?"

"Lucy—"

Nope. No service yet. Whether that was because of the basement or the storm damage, she wasn't sure. All the more reason to get out of here. She started to scoot out from under the mattress, grateful for things to do besides sit there and think about Jackson, and about losing him soon. There was so much to do, so much to clean up, so much to deal with. One big goodbye to come…

Her fingers tapped the cold concrete floor. *One, two, three. One, two, three.*

"I need to check on Mitzi," she said. "Make sure she's okay."

"Lucy, stop." He gave her a pleading look. "You need to—"

"I know, I know. I should prepare myself for the worst, just in case. I'm fine. I'll be fine. Really." It was a lie, of course. Usually when a person said everything was fine, it most certainly wasn't. But that didn't stop her from trying. Besides, there was no way Jackson could possibly know what she was going through at that moment. He wouldn't understand her emotional limbo because of him. Even if they drew this thing out between them past this day, this moment, maybe a week or two, her anxiety would catch up to her. It always did. And other people never dealt well with her issues.

Always wanting to help her. Or control her. Or, in Jackson's case, protect her.

But there wasn't anything to protect her from, because the monster lived inside her.

She was the monster.

Still, Lucy put on a brave face, because that's what she did. "I remember after Irma hit the coast of the Carolinas. The devastation. It'll be different now, though, since it's…my home…that's rubble."

"Hey," he said, reaching out to tuck her hair behind her ear. "We're alive, Lucy. That's the most important thing."

Their gazes locked. He looked good and strong and reassuring, the same as he'd been through the long, dark hours of the night.

"Yes, you're right. Thank you, Jackson."

"Don't thank me, thank Mathilda."

Mathilda didn't hold me last night.

"If you hadn't been here, though," she said, clearing her throat, "I'd have lost it a long time ago."

His expression was unreadable, and she got the distinct impression he was distancing himself from her, memorizing her, storing his time with her away.

"You wouldn't have fallen apart," he said at last. "You're strong. You do what has to be done."

Lucy looked away, determined to let him go without embarrassing either one of them. She'd known this odd thing between them was temporary going into last night, so it was good they pulled back now. Like ripping off a bandage. Besides, she'd need all her strength and concentration to deal with whatever chaos waited on the other side of the basement door.

They'd weathered a crisis together, where the line between life and death thinned to invisible proportions. That was all. And she wasn't stupid enough to think what they'd shared in the darkness would survive in the light.

"Well, the fact remains you *were* here, and I'll always be grateful for that." Without waiting for his response, she crawled out from under the mattress, then looked back at Jackson, careful to keep her demeanor and tone businesslike. "What's the best way out of here? I don't want to move the wrong thing or open the door up there and have the remainder of the house cave in on our heads."

"Let's start by getting this mattress out of the way. Scoot next to me and help me shove this half off the cages."

Lucy did so but paid a price for being close to him again. His scent and heat made her heart flutter, and she ducked to hide what had to be written all over her face. She still wanted him. Wanted to finish what she hadn't really let him start last night. She ached with the wanting.

Once they'd made short work of the mattress, she stood and massaged the pins and needles from her legs as blood flow returned to the nerve endings. From the corner of her eye, she caught Jackson wince and hop before catching his balance with a hand on the wall.

"How's your leg this morning? You should let me look at it before we go up."

"It's fine. Don't worry. I just pulled it a bit when I stood." He brushed past her and hobbled up the stairs, taking the lantern with him. "I'll check the door frame for cracks or stress fractures."

She told herself he was a grown man and could look after himself. That was easier than admitting if she touched him again, she might not let go.

"This looks sound." Jackson angled the light downward slightly then twisted the doorknob, opening the door a crack. Nothing crashed down or caved in. He turned back to her. "Ready?"

"As I'll ever be." Lucy took a deep breath and climbed up beside him.

"Hey." His voice was low, husky. Private. Without the background noise of the storm, it sounded almost...*intimate*.

But that couldn't be. He didn't want to get close to anyone. He'd made that clear. The sooner she remembered that, the better. She bowed her head for a brief moment, then looked up at him. "I'm okay. Really."

He nodded then moved away.

Shoulders squared and mind carefully blank, Lucy stepped past him into the hallway and...

Oh. My. God.

She covered her mouth and stared, barely registering the reassuring weight of Jackson's hands on her shoulders or how he pulled her stiffened body back against his. Sam scrabbled out the basement door beside her, whining and panting.

The kitchen still stood, but her office was rubble. Squashed, like some giant had stepped on it. Down the hall toward the front door, the living room looked fine. Except for the unnatural amount of light streaming down the staircase.

Holy—

Lucy took two steps in that direction, but Jackson grabbed her arm.

"Let me go first." He moved in front of her before she could stop him.

She waited in the basement doorway, one hand buried in Sam's fur to keep him where he was and safe, the other pressed to her chest, where her heart felt like it would slam out of her chest.

Rubble from what remained of the upper level of the house scattered the stairs and heaped in piles at the bottom. For the first time, the enormity of the danger they'd been in swamped her. Staying here had always been a risk. She knew that. Or thought she had.

But this...this...ripping apart one piece of her life, then sparing another, was too much.

Jackson returned and guided her toward the kitchen, hooking his fingers through Sam's collar to lead him alongside them. "Can't check it right now, too much debris. Let's get out of here. Until we see the extent of the damage from the outside, we don't know if the structure's safe, anyway."

Lucy took one last glimpse at the stairs. Hunks of roof and insulation and drywall clogged the area. Hard to tell how much of the roof had caved in, just that some if it definitely had—given the amount of light streaming in.

"Come on." He urged her forward with a tug on her hand. "Let's check on Mitzi."

Zombie-like, she took two steps, then buried her head on his shoulder. His arm came around her immediately, holding her tight to his side while Sam barked then licked her leg.

Her eyes burned, but no tears came. Maybe she was in shock. She concentrated on Jackson's solid warmth beside her and took deep, even breaths. *In, out. In, out.*

"Why does it feel like my life's ending anyway?" Whoops. She hadn't meant to ask that out loud.

"It'll be okay, Lucy," he whispered, nuzzling her ear. "Maybe not today or tomorrow, but soon. I promise."

To have done this much damage, the sheer magnitude of the storm must have been...

Mitzi.

Her head shot up. "I've got to check on her."

A sudden burst of anxiety had her pushing away from Jackson, thoughts racing. "Can you do a perimeter check while I go find out how she is?"

"No, I'll go with you," he said, his tone determined.

"I've got this," she rushed on, turning toward the kitchen. "I'll be—"

"Sam, stay." His commanding tone had her

dog sitting obediently in a small clearing of the floor.

Jackson took her hand and helped her over the rubble pile that had blown into the kitchen from what had once been her office. "Watch your step."

Lucy stepped over a chunk of debris, then froze. Her stained-glass lamp from her office. The shade was cracked, and the bulb fixture was mangled, but otherwise, it was still intact.

Her world slowly rocked back to center, filtering out some of the anxiety and OCD screaming around her edges. Her attention zeroed to the here and now. There'd be plenty of time later to sort out her feelings about everything that had happened. She set the lamp on the untouched kitchen table and tightened her hold on Jackson's hand. He felt like a lifeline, one she could use.

"Help me get the bars off the door?" he asked, his tone quiet and calm.

She was grateful for the task. Even the smallest chore meant progress, that the worst was over and every step, no matter how tiny, was a step away from this…this…

Jackson shuddered and she frowned, dropping his hand. "Do you want the mop for a crutch again?"

"Nah. It feels better this morning." At her dubious look, he grinned. "Really. I guess last night's enforced rest was good for something after all."

She didn't want to think about last night right now. Not if she wanted to keep it together.

He was still limping a little, favoring his wounded thigh, but he could walk. She turned her attention to the door and what lay beyond. Or rather, who.

"Let me push, then you pull," he directed. "It's warped a bit."

Five minutes later the bars were removed, and the door swung open, revealing the vacant spot where her screened-in porch had once been.

Her mind registered the incredible amount of debris, both natural and man-made, littering the compound, but most of her attention was focused on the pond.

Lucy searched for a safe path through the rubble while Jackson went back inside, scooped up all sixty pounds of whining Sam in his arms and carried him out into the backyard with them, setting him down before motioning for her to follow.

After waiting for Sam to do his business, she left him with Jackson while she continued on toward the pond.

"At least there's no flooding," she called over her shoulder. Downed trees and limbs and more chunks of her roof blocked her path. She headed in what appeared to be the most direct route around it all.

A bark sounded behind her, and she stopped again to look back at Jackson and Sam.

"Seagull," he yelled. "Go on, we'll catch up."

Lucy nodded, deliberately not looking past him to her house. Not now. Mitzi first, then the rest. The house wasn't going anywhere. At least what was left of it.

The egg mound. If it was waterlogged,

the hatchlings would die. The sky was still overcast, but the rain and wind had stopped. Still, it could flood. Big Pine Key was small, and a storm of Mathilda's ferocity had likely wreaked havoc on the tides, too. "Please," she prayed. "No more."

Lucy rounded a twisted piece of what had once been her storage shed and finally got her first good look at the pond. Swollen past its banks, the water had stopped several feet shy of infiltrating the egg mound. Mitzi was nowhere to be seen.

She broke into a run and didn't stop running until she was halfway around the pond. A dark shadow floated in the shallows. Lucy positioned herself to get the best view without antagonizing the gator. Having her binoculars would've helped, but they'd been in her office, which was gone. The sense of loss blindsided her again, stealing her breath for a long, painful moment.

Then, as if summoned from her fervent wishes, large, warm hands covered her shoulders again.

"Breathe," Jackson said from behind her.

She hadn't even heard him come up. "Is Mitzi okay?"

"I haven't seen her move yet, but she's near the mound, and it doesn't look damaged or flooded, from what I can tell."

"How will you know for sure?"

She tore her gaze away from Mitzi and faced Jackson. Her heart skipped. She liked looking at him, looking *to* him. "Mostly observation. I'll have to get closer if she seems to be suffering. As for the nestlings, they're due to hatch in about two weeks. We'll know for certain then." She glanced around. "Where's Sam?"

"I found a leash in the clinic—which is fine, by the way," he said, watching her closely. "I cleared an area for him and left him tethered near the porch."

"Okay," she said finally, for lack of anything better to say, unable to handle his scrutiny with her control so thinly stretched. "What?"

"You." He ran a finger down her cheek.

"What about me?" *Dumb question.*

"I've never met anyone like you. Strong, tough, courageous."

"You're an EMT. You work with strong, tough, courageous people every day."

"Not like you." His mouth tipped up into a crooked smile and his eyes lit up, banishing all the darkness. She couldn't help smiling back, despite the circumstances. "You're different."

"In a good way, I hope." *Stop it. You don't need his attention. You don't need anyone.*

Then he was kissing her again, and there was no time to breathe, no time to think, no time to worry. Passion pushed her, drove her, tested her. And she wanted more, *needed* so much more.

Lucy stood in his arms, helpless against the yearning.

Helpless.

Something deep inside her clicked. Or maybe it snapped. And the whirling maelstrom of emotions she'd kept locked away for so long crashed past her barriers. Violent, powerful, the force flowing through her, energizing her. Revitalizing her.

She moved against him, pulled at him, kissed him back, arched against him. She didn't think, she didn't wonder, she just acted.

Jackson gave as good as he got, each of them fighting for control.

Now she didn't feel helpless, didn't feel broken.

Now she felt like the woman he'd described. Strong. Tough. Courageous.

Then, as swiftly as it had swept over them, the storm receded. Their kisses gentled, slowed, until they stood looking at each other.

"Thank you," she whispered past the constriction in her throat.

His gaze betrayed him. His walls, his defenses were gone. At last she saw behind them. Saw his pain, sadness, wariness. But there was also fierce strength, honor and faith.

And a banked fire that had nothing to do with protection. Her knees buckled.

Jackson's arms tightened around her, and the flickering heat in his eyes threatened to erupt into an inferno. Intimacy. Not just physical, but in far more dangerous ways—mental, emotional.

The imaginary thread they'd forged between them the night before flared brighter. Irreversible as any physical bond. Maybe more so. She couldn't have felt any more open or vulnerable if he'd stripped her naked, pulled her down and driven himself into her right on the hard, wet ground.

Jackson cupped her cheeks and rested his forehead against hers. "Don't thank me. It's not me, Lucy. It's you. It's always been you."

He was wrong. It wasn't her. It wasn't him, either. It was them.

He kissed her, sweet and short, then stepped back and held out his hand, his weight shifting unevenly on his wounded leg. "Ready?"

"Yes." She cast a swift glance at Mitzi. Then did a double take. "She's at the egg mound!"

"Good." Jackson grinned. "Let's go check out your clinic. I think it's okay, but you should check."

"Right. I need to know what resources I have available. Maybe I'll finally have some luck and Mitzi won't need my help." She didn't let herself think about the nestlings.

There was nothing she could do for them at this point anyway except wait. "Once we make sure the clinic's okay, we can bring the rest of the animals up from the basement."

Lucy unhooked Sam's leash from the porch then walked with Jackson to the clinic with him. He took her hand again and fell into step beside her like he belonged there. And it seemed the most natural thing in the world to shorten her stride to accommodate his limp.

CHAPTER TWELVE

SEVERAL HOURS HAD passed by the time she and Jackson had moved Bubba and King from the basement to the clinic, then finished a rough categorization of the damage. It hadn't been easy. Several times, usually just when she thought she was handling things pretty well, she'd find something—a broken chunk of equipment or a twisted piece of furniture—and the overwhelming depth of her predicament would threaten to consume her. And each time Jackson was there. Sometimes with a steady look, sometimes with a touch, and sometimes with a quick, tight hug.

She might have been able to handle all this without him, but it would've been so much worse. And she didn't beat herself up over taking the solace he offered. He'd be gone soon enough anyway, then she'd have plenty of time to shoulder the burden alone.

In the meantime, she absorbed as much of his strength as he was willing to give, storing it up for later. For all the times he wouldn't be there, for all the times when she might wish he was.

"I think this is the last of it." Jackson entered the main treatment room, which they'd turned into a sort of inventory center. He had a small box under one arm and a large green trash bag in the other hand. "I was able to get service out on the edge of the compound. Talked to Luis on the phone. Key West came through the hurricane okay—some damage and flooding there, too. He'll send help for us as soon as he can, but it could be a while."

She nodded and went back to her work, cataloging supplies. Fortunately, Jackson had been right. Her clinic had been relatively untouched, only a few roof shingles swept away. The chain-link pens outside and a good portion of the fence surrounding the property had been twisted or destroyed, but replacing them was the least of her concerns.

Lucy hadn't missed the strain on Jackson's face, either, or how pronounced his limp had become again. He'd taken more pain meds earlier and even let her check the stitches. There was some redness, but it actually looked okay. His endurance was admirable, but there was a limit, even for him.

"I think we've done enough," she said, putting a dish of wet food into King's cage then shutting the door, doing her best to keep her voice casual to gain his compliance. "Why don't you take a break and lie down on the cot in the back room?"

"You stay out here some nights?" he asked, ignoring her suggestion. She'd thought after last night and their kiss by the pond maybe they'd gotten past his superhero complex, but apparently not.

She shrugged. "Some animals need regular attention, so it makes sense for me to stay close by."

"Hmm." He hefted the bag onto the long counter then folded his arms atop of it. "You give so much to your work, Lucy. Is there any left for yourself?"

"I love what I do." She picked up her clipboard, not meeting his gaze. "Go on. Lie down for a bit. Take some weight off that leg. Doctor's orders. I can inventory the rest of this stuff by myself."

Instead of doing as she asked, however, he grabbed a stool and took a seat, propping his leg on a box on the floor in front of him. "Satisfied?"

More than she ever thought possible. She liked his company, liked having him nearby, where she could see him whenever she wanted.

When she didn't answer, he continued. "I never asked, but it must be tough financing an operation like this. How do you do it? Grants? Private funding? Donations?"

"I manage," she said, hoping he'd let the topic drop. The last thing she wanted to do was discuss her financial situation, mainly because that would lead to more talk of her past, and she didn't want to get into all that again when everything was going so well now.

"Do you ever travel to help animals?" he asked, thankfully changing subjects. "Luis used to go on mission trips, helping under-privileged kids and adults by giving them life-saving medical care. I've heard of vets doing free spay and neuter surgeries and stuff, too."

"Sometimes," Lucy said, doing her best to concentrate on the crate of supplies she was counting, and failing. "But I don't travel. I have the patients that need my help flown in here free of charge so I can give them treatment here at the compound. Your brother, Luis, sounds like a good man."

"He is." He nodded, his crooked smile emerging again. "Though he can be difficult, too, like you."

She shot him a look. "I'm not difficult."

"Sweetheart, you're like herding cats at a rodeo." At her scowl, he chuckled. "But in the best way."

Lucy blushed as his laugh deepened.

"I meant it as a compliment," he said, taking her hand again. "You're complex. I like that."

Robert had always claimed Lucy was complex, too. But in all the wrong ways. Ways he felt compelled to fix whether she wanted him to or not. Her hackles rose. No, the last thing she needed was another man trying to take over her life, thinking he knew best. And while she cared about Jackson, more than she ever had about anyone, she'd fought too hard to let him steal her freedom, no matter how adorable he might be.

Jackson saw her close him out as effectively as the basement had shut out Hurricane Mathilda.

"Listen," Lucy said, the edge in her words telling him things were most definitely not fine at all. "About last night. And about what happened at the pond earlier. I think we should forget it. All of it."

"And if I don't want to?" he shot back. He cared, for reasons he didn't want to contemplate too deeply at the moment. Usually he never had to deal with the morning-after awkwardness because he always made sure he was long gone by then. They hadn't even had sex, not really. Just fooled around. They'd both liked it. He'd thought maybe they'd continue down that path earlier, but it seemed he'd been wrong. Again.

"Why not?" She set her clipboard aside and crossed her arms. "I'd think you'd be over-joyed. No strings, just like you wanted. So, why are fighting this?"

"I'm not." *Liar.* He gestured toward the rest of the room. "I just figured we'd enjoy each other's company a little longer until help arrives. Get to know each other better."

"I know enough about you already."

His hackles rose at that. What the hell? She'd been fine last night, having him close, holding her, touching her, kissing her. Now she wanted him gone. He leaned forward, jaw tight. "Really? Because I don't feel like I know you at all, Lucy. One minute you're cowering against me, holding on for dear life, the next you can't push me away fast enough. Sorry, but I don't go hot and cold that fast. And while we're at it, where in the hell did you get this idea that you have to do every-thing yourself and accepting any help or ad-vice makes you weak? This is one battle you don't have to fight alone."

"What do you know about my battles, Jackson?" She turned away, and in the past, Jackson would've let her go, but today he couldn't. Wouldn't. He knew more about fighting demons and pain and being alone than she'd learn in two lifetimes. He didn't give an inch.

"I know you've been hurt. I know someone probably thought they were helping, and instead they nearly broke you, but you're still here. You're a survivor." Unexpected anger constricted his throat, but he forced the words out, anyway. "I am, too. But we all need help, Lucy."

"Not me. And you're one to talk," she said, her tone defensive. "You don't let others do for you, either. You didn't even want me to take care of a simple thigh wound last night." Lucy snorted and shook her head. "You're an EMT, Jackson. You know better than anyone how quickly a cut like that can get infected. But instead of worrying about yourself, you're acting like rescuing me is a personal crusade or something. You came onto my property and tried to take over. Don't tell me—"

One second he was sitting on the stool, the

next it crashed to the tile floor as he took her in his arms, his face inches from hers. "Stop trying to figure me out, Lucy. You won't get it right. But you were correct about one thing. Being here *is* a crusade for me. I save people. It's what I do. Who I am. And I take that responsibility seriously." He drew her closer until barely a whisper separated them. "The reason I asked about your money situation is because I've got contacts in the area. They might be willing to help you get back on your feet. Not because I think you can't do it for yourself. I know you can." He narrowed his gaze. "So, why don't you tell me why you're really shoving me away?"

She struggled against his hold. "Because when people try to help, they end up taking over, and I can't afford to lose control of my life again. I won't. That's why I don't need your help or anyone else's."

"So that's it? You close yourself off and only open up around your animals?"

"They respect my boundaries, which is more than I can say for everyone else I've ever—"

"Loved?" he broke in, sensing he was getting close to her truth.

She opened her mouth, closed it, then opened it again.

"Tell me."

"Why?" she shouted. "It's over with. Done. I've been hurt and I won't let it happen again, Jackson. I've had my emotions, my issues, used to control me, all under the guise of help. So, no. I don't want it and I don't need it. Not from you or anyone else. Understand?" An angry sob broke through. "I won't let you in. I won't let you that close again. I can't."

He pulled her into a tight embrace, tucking her head against his chest and resting his cheek atop of her head, running his other hand up and down her back. Her pain and fear broke his soul.

"Shh. I shouldn't have pushed like that." He kissed her hair, then pressed another to her temple. "I know what it's like to love so much it hurts, then be betrayed by those who were supposed to care for you." He tilted her face upward, forcing her to look at him then placed a soft kiss on her lips. "And I'm a bastard for badgering you. It's none of my business."

"No, it's not." She sniffled, a tear trickling down her cheek. He traced it away with his thumb. "I like my life now just the way it is, Jackson. I have my work. I have my animals. Simple. Steady. Safe. I'd think you of all people would get that. Simple. Safe. Steady. But now...with you..."

He cursed under his breath, then held her gaze. "I want to help you, Lucy, not change you. No strings, no payback. Nothing. I just want to help. Please let me."

She trembled, and his chest squeezed with an odd mix of desire and dread. Desire to hold her, protect her, care for her. Dread because he knew she might not let him. Not now, not ever.

Forty-eight hours ago, he wouldn't have cared. Now he did.

More than he wanted to admit, and it rocked him to his core. As much as she feared letting him in, the thought of opening his heart to her terrified him even more. Because the one thing he wanted more than anything in the world now—true closeness, true intimacy, with Lucy—was probably the very last thing she'd give him.

"I can't, Jackson," she said at last, her voice still thick with unshed tears.

"Can't or won't?"

Frustrated, Jackson hobbled back to the counter, righted his stool, then took a seat again. The last thing he wanted to do with her today was fight, so he tried a different tack. "What about the money?"

"I don't need money. I could buy and sell this place five times over."

He blinked at her a moment. That was news. "I didn't realize being a vet paid that well."

"It doesn't. It's family money."

"You're loaded then, huh?" He'd meant it as a joke, but she didn't smile.

Honestly, he didn't care if she owned the entire state of Florida. Money didn't impress him. Never had. But if it made her more secure and happy, he was all for it.

"My grandmother married well. She left me a sizable amount in a trust fund." She stared at the center of his chest, burning a hole through it. "I only use it for the clinic and facilities. There's plenty to fix this place, even expand if I wanted, but…"

The unspoken reason made him rock back slightly on the legs of his stool. "But then you'd have to hire staff, maybe take on a partner. And you don't want to do that."

From the way her pretty face blanched, he knew he'd hit a bull's-eye.

She bit her lip. "Don't judge me."

"I wasn't."

Lucy frowned. "Why did you really become a paramedic, Jackson? Why not a doctor, like Luis?" He opened his mouth to respond, but she talked over him. "I think it's because as an EMT you get to take control and assess the situation, then turn the patients over to someone else without ever getting too close. You leave them before they can leave you." At his stunned silence, she nodded. "That's it, isn't it?"

He did his best to shut down his reaction, to choke the burning bile in his gut. She'd hit far too close to the mark for his comfort. Rather than confirm her suspicions, however, he snorted and looked away. "What a pair we are."

Her shoulders slumped. "Sorry?"

He exhaled slowly, then walked over and pulled her to him again. She went easily, sliding her arms around his waist and resting her cheek over his heart. Jackson spoke into her hair, "Yes, we are. Both of us. Sorry to the core."

"When I turned eighteen, I was supposed to get access to the money in my trust fund," she said against his skin. "But my parents didn't think I could handle it, because of my OCD and anxiety. For a long time, I bought into their idea that I was helpless. Of course, it didn't help that my ex supported that theory, too. Robert always treated me like a live grenade about to go off. I think the only reason he wanted to marry me was the money. Well, that and to use me for his graduate study work."

Tension knotted the muscles between his shoulder blades. The thought of anyone abusing Lucy's trust like that made his blood boil.

Still, she needed to get this out, and he needed to listen. "Go on."

She inhaled deep. "Robert and I dated for six months and were engaged twice as long. At first it was nice, his constant pampering and protection. But as time went on, it became suffocating. Like it had been growing up with my parents, only a million times worse. Then, one day I walked in on him discussing my case with the dean of his department—anonymously, of course—like I was some lab rat and not his beloved fiancée. He was asking for advice on how to handle me going forward, so our marriage didn't contaminate his research. That was the last straw.

"I decided then and there to leave. I'd been volunteering at a local shelter for a while by that point, and when Dr. Dave offered to help me get into vet school, I jumped at the chance. He wrote me letters of recommendation and even helped me get a couple of scholarships, since I still couldn't access my trust fund at that point. After I graduated, I got lawyers and sued to access my money. Once I won the lawsuit, I bought this place and never looked back. It's taken me a long time to find my freedom. I don't ever want to lose it again. Now do you understand why this place is so important to me and why I had to stay?"

"I do." He gently lifted her chin with his finger, his stomach sinking. "You're happy here, alone?"

"I am." She raised her head, her dark gaze determined. "Here, I have control over my own destiny. I've put my past behind me and moved forward. I won't leave that behind. Even for a hurricane."

Jackson understood. Deep in his bones, he got it. It was both a blessing and a curse, because her triumph was his defeat.

He had no right to expect more from her, because last night had been nothing but two lost, lonely souls holding on for dear life during an emergency. Just affirming life during a disaster. Nothing more, nothing less. He needed to let it go, let her go and move on.

Because that's what he did.

"You know what I think?" he asked, forcing a smile he didn't feel. "I think it's their loss.

I think if they couldn't see all the wonderful potential in you, then screw them."

Lucy chuckled. "And are you talking from personal experience?"

His jaw clenched, a muscle ticking in his cheek. He could tell her about himself, about being abandoned by his own mother, by the one person who should've never left, about being unworthy of love, but what would be the point? It was water under the bridge. Literally. So, he gave her a half-truth instead. "I have some experience with being disappointed by the people you love, yeah." An image of the photo he'd found in her office the day before flashed in his head, and he let her go to rummage in the trash bag to find it. "Hey, I found something of yours yesterday, before we went down to the basement."

"What?" Her dark brows drew together.

"A photo, from your office. Since you didn't have it out, I wasn't sure whether it was something you'd want to save—"

He handed it to Lucy, and her expression shifted from happy to sad to resigned in ten seconds flat. The same emotions he experienced whenever he saw a rare picture of himself with his birth mom. There weren't many reminders left from those days before the Durands had taken him in, but the ones that had made it packed a hell of a wallop.

"Oh God," she whispered. Then she was back in his arms, hugging him tight. When she pulled away, he recognized the same vulnerability in her that he'd fought against his whole life. "This is Robert."

Jackson nodded, keeping his expression blank while his breath lodged painfully in his lungs, the pain of loneliness, abandonment, threatening to overtake him if he wasn't careful. He let her go, then shoved his hands in his pockets to hide their tremble. "I'm sorry."

Tears burned in her eyes once more. "It's okay."

The defeat in her tone hurt his heart, but he couldn't respond. Couldn't tell her what he was feeling, because he didn't understand it himself. If he did, he'd be forced to let her in, and if that happened, it would break him down, and he might never be able to build his walls up again. So, instead, he kissed her, his mouth fierce as his heart shattered inside him.

Then he was holding her again, touching her, because he needed to, needed her more than he needed his next breath. His hands cupped her cheeks then trailed down her arms, her skin hot and soft under his searching fingertips. She dropped the photo to clutch at the open edges of his shirt, pulling it off his body. Jackson let it fall, along with the rest of the tattered barriers around his heart, and claimed her mouth again, his desire for her evident in every touch and caress. Needing, wanting, more and more. He explored every inch of her, first with fingers, then with lips and tongue, desperate and worshipful, knowing this first time might be their last.

He nuzzled the side of her neck, breathing her name against her ear. "Sweet Lucy."

She opened her eyes, then leaned in and kissed his nipple. He bucked beneath her, couldn't help it, his deep groan vibrating beneath her mouth. She stopped and looked up at him, questioning.

"No," he rasped. "Feels…wonderful."

She smiled, and a bit more of his control slipped away. It was so easy for her to distract him, disarm him, and damn if he could bring himself to care. The sudden lifting of the burden he'd carried for so long too heady to resist. She kissed her way across his chest to his other nipple and teased him again. His hips rose against hers, leaving little doubt how badly he wanted this, wanted her. His body felt on fire, his blood singing in his veins and his erection so hard it hurt. He had more experience than a man should, but it had never, ever been like this before. Like he'd die if he couldn't satisfy this hunger, this craving, this need for Lucy that pushed him, drove him, controlled him.

Then, suddenly, his hands were on her, tugging at her shirt. Humid Florida air moved across his bare skin, electrifying it. The feel of her breasts in his palms was wild, erotic. He wanted to make her feel good, feel precious. When her shirt was gone, he wanted more. Wanted his hands all over her. His mouth and tongue, too.

She seemed to feel the same urgency as

she touched him right back, seeking her own pleasure.

He groaned, and her hands stilled. She tried to cover herself, but he stopped her.

"Don't. Please. You're so beautiful." Her dark eyes still glimmered with a hint of insecurity, and Jackson reassured her. "Please, Lucy. Let me see you. Let me be with you."

She did, and his wanting burned brighter, hotter. He hadn't thought it possible, but he'd been wrong.

"Perfect. That's what you are, Lucy." His hands moved lower, and her breath turned shallow. He stopped at the button on the waistband of her jeans, same as he'd done the night before, praying she wouldn't stop him this time. "Okay?"

She bit her lip, then gave a shy nod. "Yes. Please."

Jackson undid the button then lowered her zip one notch at a time. "No need to beg, sweetheart. Unless you want to…"

CHAPTER THIRTEEN

LUCY LIFTED HER hips to help him remove her jeans and panties, then waited as he took off his own. They were both naked now, and he leaned back against the wall again, his casual pose saying he was completely comfortable in his own skin. She wondered what that was like.

"Come here," he beckoned, his voice rough with desire. "Touch me, Lucy. Wherever you want. I'm yours."

She reached out tentatively and grasped his hard length. Hot, satiny, rigid, the skin so soft. He jerked in her hand, and her core clenched in response. If she got on her knees, she could take him in her mouth and...

Her intentions must've shown on her face, because he said, "Please."

So, she did, her world reduced to this man,

this moment, the feel and taste of him on her tongue. No worries, no anxiety, no regrets.

As she tightened her lips around his shaft, he slipped his fingers through her hair, not forcing but guiding her gently to show her what he liked. Never in her life had she felt this free, brought to such a simple common denominator. One thing. Only one, that she wanted more than her next breath.

Lucy slid her mouth slowly off him and felt his shaking groan in the depths of her soul. It echoed inside her, matching her own passion. Her gaze traveled up his taut abdomen, across his chest, to his clenched jaw, his beautiful compressed mouth, then finally to his eyes.

And there she found everything she'd ever wanted.

She had no idea what to say. She didn't have to say anything.

"There's a condom in my wallet, back pocket of my pants." His words were rough, uncivilized. And exactly what she wanted to hear.

Without looking away from him, she fumbled beside her for his balled-up pants and pulled out the tiny foil packet. Her fingers fumbled to open it then smooth it onto his hard length. Damn if it wasn't erotic as hell.

Then Jackson leaned forward and lifted her. She wrapped her arms around his neck and her legs around his hips until she straddled him. Lucy did her best not to knock against his injured leg, but any concerns she had about that disappeared as she slowly sank down onto him inch by delicious inch. His gaze stayed locked on hers until he filled her completely, so deep she wasn't sure where he started and she ended. It was wondrous, magnificent. A bit uncomfortable at first, then her body adjusted and...

"Stop thinking." He turned them so her upper back was against the cool wall of the clinic, his arms supporting her, then he leaned forward to nuzzle her neck, not moving yet. His hot breath fanned her face as he whispered, "Relax."

He massaged her hips until she did so, then cupped her breasts.

Lucy gasped and rocked forward. The motion made her moan. Jackson bucked, then stilled almost immediately. "Sorry. Did I hurt you?"

"No." He slid a bit farther into her, and she whimpered, not from pain but from pleasure. Lucy clung to him, digging her nails into his shoulders as he nipped her earlobe.

Then they moved together, the tightly coiled need inside her unwinding. Her body took over with a single-minded intensity that sent any thought but completion spiraling away.

Jackson controlled the rhythm. She moved, he followed. Her movements became wild, frenzied, exulting in his sleek, powerful body that matched her thrust for thrust.

Then she was there. On the brink of orgasm.

He stroked her most sensitive flesh, sending her flying over the edge. The world exploded into shards of light behind her closed eyelids, like tiny firecrackers going off in every nerve ending in her body. And in the center of it all, Jackson shouted her name and found his own release.

Afterward, Lucy collapsed against him, chest heaving, skin damp, pulse pounding.

For the first time in forever, she couldn't think. Didn't want to think. Hadn't gotten over feeling yet. Feeling freer than she'd ever been before, all because she'd allowed this man to take control.

Somewhere in the back of her mind, a warning bell sounded, but she was far too blissed out to care at that moment.

Jackson smoothed the tangled hair away from her face, his fingers still shaking from the force of his own climax. Then he kissed her. He'd meant it to be gentle, short, sweet. But he couldn't stop. He kept his lips on hers as their breathing slowed and their hearts returned to normal rhythms.

Sleepiness lurked around his edges, but he resisted. He wanted to stay here, connected to her like this, forever.

And then it hit him. A force as violent as the hurricane that had ripped apart her house.

He'd let her in. Past his walls and barriers and safeguards. And he *never* did that.

Until today.

He closed his eyes and rested his forehead

against the base of her neck. He shouldn't still be here. No. He should get up, get dressed, get gone like he always did after sex. Sleeping with someone meant the end of the affair, not the beginning of something more.

Then his lips touched her pulse point and another, more startling realization struck.

He wasn't leaving…because he didn't want to.

Holy hell.

His eyes flew open, and Lucy shifted away. "Jackson, this… I feel… We need…"

She tried to pull away, but his arms tightened around her.

"No. Don't. Not yet. We'll have to talk about this, but not now, okay? Let me be here."

"Jackson—" She frowned, going still.

"Please." He couldn't explain it to her, because he didn't understand it himself yet. "Just let me…stay here with you…for a little while longer."

A small eternity passed before she relaxed again, and a fierce, unexpected contentment filled him. He gazed down at her, never imagining he'd hold a woman like Lucy.

Didn't want to think about what would happen later...

Then the unmistakable sound of a helicopter cut into his thoughts.

Dammit.

Seemed later was closer than he'd thought. And getting closer by the second.

Sam woke up from where he'd been sleeping by the door and started barking. King meowed, and Bubba danced back and forth on his perch, squawking, "Wanted dead or alive."

Lucy lifted her head from his chest, her dark brows knitting together. "Is that the help that was on the way?"

"Probably," Jackson muttered, for once damning his brother's hyperefficiency.

He let her go reluctantly, then dragged his pants on and located his buttonless shirt while Lucy dressed as well. Awkward silence fell between them, and before he could break it, she was out the door calling to him over her shoulder, "I'm going to check on Mitzi again."

Not exactly how he'd wanted their interlude to end.

She'd finally let him in, let him close, and now it was like she couldn't get away from him fast enough. Old doubts and fears clawed awake inside him, but he shoved them aside. No, that wasn't what was happening here. They'd both needed to be ready when help arrived, that's all. He was reading too much into it. His feelings were still too new, too raw, too confusing. Jackson paused in the doorway, watching as a medevac chopper moved toward the front corner of the compound diagonally across from the pond, the only place with enough free space to land among the debris.

Limping, he headed across the littered grounds, doing his best to convince himself that this was good. Instead of being disappointed about this sudden turn of events, he should be delighted. Help was in that helicopter. He and Lucy could get things straightened out here, then he could go back to Key West. They'd talk again later. Sort it all out. Decide where to go from here.

It was all good. He didn't have to fear connection. Things wouldn't turn out like they had before.

He wouldn't be abandoned again.

Except as the helicopter swooped in, wind from the rotors whipping Lucy's hair around her face and rippling the hem of her tank top, this all seemed like more of a dream. A fever dream.

But would reality break the fever?

He stopped several feet behind Lucy, not certain she knew he was there.

His old doubts and fears dug their claws into him, growing in his gut with each beat of his heart until it felt like they might strangle him. He'd been through a lot in his life, more than most, but it felt like nothing had prepared him for this. Not his rescues in the coast guard. Not all the life-and-death situations he faced on a daily basis. Not losing his birth mom all those years ago.

As Lucy continued to shut him out, he knew nothing had prepared him for the very real possibility that he might well lose her in the next couple of minutes. And the worst part was, there wasn't a damned thing he could do about it.

Because he'd gone into it knowing how much she valued her freedom and how hard she'd fight to keep it. Just as hard as he'd had to battle to let her in. And in that kind of war, could there be a winner?

The chopper's huge rotors slowed, and the wind died down. Finally, the small hatch door opened, and the pilot climbed out and ran up to them. "Dr. Lucy Miller?"

"Yes, that's me," she said, shaking his hand. "Thanks for coming."

"It's my duty, ma'am," the pilot said, turning to Jackson next. "Got here as soon as I could."

After getting a rundown on the conditions in Key West and the surrounding area, he gave the pilot a quick tour of the compound while Lucy checked on Mitzi. Jackson had thought he'd feel worse about surrendering the IC spot, but honestly, he didn't care at the moment. Maybe because of the ordeal they'd been through. Maybe because of their brush with death. Or maybe because of the weird pressure in his chest urging him to head straight back to Lucy's side and stay there forever, consequences be damned.

But he couldn't do that. Lucy didn't want that. He didn't want that, either.

Do I?

Hands fisted at his sides, Jackson flashed the pilot a hard smile he hoped passed as normal and listened to what he was saying.

"Most of the problems in Key West came from flooding. The governor has declared a state of emergency, at least, so we can start getting federal aid in to help in the cleanup efforts." The guy took off his sunglasses and rubbed his eyes, dark shadows beneath them from lack of sleep. Jackson hadn't looked in a mirror yet that day, but he figured he probably looked much the same. "Looks like you guys were hit hard here, too. Hopefully, this will all work out and we get the funding we need to start repairs sooner rather than later, but with FEMA you never know..."

Lucy walked up to them then, distracting Jackson again. Her expression was remote again, unreadable, and he wished to hell he knew how to crack her code, because the less he knew about how this was going to go, the more his inner control freak went wild. What if she didn't want him to stay? What if instead of bringing them closer together, making love earlier had only proved to her that he wasn't the man for her? Sure, it had been great. Universe-altering, at least for him. But Lucy was a closed book now, one he desperately wished he could decipher.

"I'm sure you need to get back to work," she said, jarring him out of his thoughts.

The pilot checked his watch. "Yep, I do. I've got room for one cage onboard and one adult, whoever's ready to go."

"You should take King back with you," Lucy said, turning away. "He's healing well and is ready to foster."

He frowned. "I'm sorry?"

She headed back into the clinic. "When you go back to Key West, take King with you."

"I'm not going back." He shook his head and followed her into the clinic, not wanting to discuss things in front of the pilot. "Not yet. We've got things to talk about, Lucy. Things feel different now."

"Different how?"

His chest itched as the emotional demons inside him tried harder to claw their way out. He rubbed the area over his heart, more than aware of the pilot waiting outside the door. Now wasn't the time and this wasn't the place. He needed space to figure all this out so he didn't do something stupid like fall to his knees and beg her to let him stay, let him help, let him into her heart and her life.

A muscle ticked in his tense cheek, and he looked away from her, old pain and new fears blotting out the light from their earlier lovemaking. *No. Not lovemaking. Don't call it that. Don't put too much meaning into it. Don't start thinking you're worthy of more than just sex.*

She was not going to keep him. A black pit of despair swirled inside him, swallowing up everything, including his patience. He waved her off and turned away before she caught the devastation lurking just beneath his surface.

This. This was exactly why he kept his distance, kept his guard up.

Things didn't change. Because he didn't deserve them to change.

"Forget it. It doesn't matter." He turned away and walked over to King's cage, staring in at the tiny kitten and feeling the same embarrassment and grief and loss he'd felt when he'd watched his birth mother's taillights disappear from view for the last time. King meowed and crawled over to the front of the cage as if to offer his support. "You're right. I should head home. Lots of important things to get done," he said quietly, doing his best to rebuild his shattered defenses before it was too late. "And I'll take the kitten with me, like you wanted."

"Great." She paused, ignoring the darkening scowl on Jackson's face, because if she didn't, she'd end up getting swallowed up by the memories of them together earlier, and she couldn't handle that. Not right now. Those moments with him had been incredible, some of the most intense in her life. And while she probably should regret them, she couldn't. Never would, honestly, given how miserable the coming days ahead would be without him. She swallowed hard against the sudden constriction in her throat. "Get back to your team. Your life in Key West. I've got plenty to do here to keep me busy. Goodbye, Jackson."

She was getting her freedom back, just like she'd wanted.

Lucy thought she'd feel better about that than she did.

Rather than stand there and wallow in her sadness, she walked outside again and headed for the pond, then stopped and looked back at the pilot, eyes burning. She blinked hard. She would not cry now. No. "Jackson will be riding with you, along with a kitten. Thanks again for coming."

Near the pond, she watched as the pilot and Jackson got King's cage and IV apparatus loaded into the back of the helicopter, then looked away again as Jackson hobbled over to her.

"You sure you're okay here alone?" Jackson asked, taking her arm gently.

She pulled free, not looking up at him. Hard enough having him near now without him touching her, too. No. If this was the end, then it was best to get on with it. Like ripping off a bandage. Sam whined from where he stayed glued to her ankle. "No. But I will be."

She'd be great, as soon as she got back inside, got back on her schedule. Whenever life went south, her routines got her through. Waking up at the same time every morning, counting her steps, arranging the shirts in her closet and remotes on her coffee table. Arranging all the things in our house "just so." Working with Sam every day. Avoiding cracks in the sidewalk. Turning knobs. Walking to the beat of the ticking clock in her living room.

Except her house was gone. There were no more knobs, no more clocks, no more Jackson.

She swallowed hard, anxiety gouging away at what little peace she had left from their lovemaking. When she'd been with him, last night and this morning, all those tics and troubles had disappeared. Now that he was leaving again, though, they rushed back like a tsunami, despite her meds.

That was bad. Very bad indeed.

She needed to get inside, get away from all this stress, get herself and her life back on track again.

You can do this. You're in control.

The pilot yelled from the cockpit door. "Sir. I'm happy to fly you back, but I've got other runs, so we'll need to leave now."

Jackson kept his attention riveted on her. "Lucy?"

His voice roughened, almost like he regretted leaving. She hazarded a glance at him, searching his face for clues to how he felt but found none. In the end, she couldn't ask him to stay. They'd both said they wanted no strings, no promises, no complications. She wouldn't go back on that now, even if getting her freedom back meant her heart would be tied to Jackson forever.

How ironic.

"Go. Don't worry about me," she croaked. "I have enough supplies to last me for a while. I'll be just fine by myself. The way I like it."

Jackson's expression remained inscrutable. Then, after a long moment, he seemed to come to a decision, signaling to the pilot, who started the rotors up again.

Right. Okay. This was it. Jackson was leaving. She'd likely never spend time with him like this again. He could easily have a vet in Key West do checkups on the kitten and probably would. Less messy that way. Best make this as easy as possible. No tears or long, uncomfortable goodbyes. After all, they'd only met a few days prior. And they'd had sex not thirty minutes prior. Her chest ached.

Lucy trembled under his continued scrutiny. If he didn't leave soon, this wasn't going to be clean. Her emotions were too close to the surface, too choppy, like the still churning waters of the Gulf offshore.

God, please let me end this without humiliating myself.

Then she was in his arms, and he was kissing her. No. Not a kiss. A claiming, a branding with his taste, his textures, his touch. And at the exact moment she felt her knees wobble, he let her go.

"I know you want me gone," Jackson said roughly. "I'm sorry I wasn't what you needed. I'm sorry I wasn't better for you."

Before she could respond and tell him no, that wasn't true, he was everything she'd ever wanted and more, it was her that was wrong, her that was the problem, Jackson traced a finger across her lower lip, silencing her.

"Goodbye, Lucy," Jackson said, then turned and hobbled to the waiting helicopter.

CHAPTER FOURTEEN

JACKSON WALKED INTO the ER at Key West General and headed over to where his brother stood at the nurses' station going through patient files.

It had been two weeks since Hurricane Mathilda had roared through the Keys, and they were still picking up the pieces. The team had done a fantastic job, following the outlined plans he'd given them before heading north, and the area was recovering nicely.

As far as his own property went, his houseboat had survived the storm pretty much unscathed, except for a few minor dings and some flooding. His truck hadn't fared as well, sustaining major damage from a downed tree at the compound, but his insurance company was handling that and had towed the vehicle away without him having to make another trip to Big Pine Key.

Which was good, because he still had no idea what the hell to do about Lucy. He knew from the cleaning crew he'd sent to help her that she was alive and well and rebuilding like the rest of the residents in the area. What he didn't know, however, was if she regretted how they'd ended things as much as he did and if she'd ever give him another chance to prove himself.

I'm sorry I wasn't what you needed. I'm sorry I wasn't better for you...

"Feeling better?" Luis asked without looking up at him. "Mr. Regional Director."

"Yeah." *Nah.* Jackson shrugged, a vain attempt to relieve some of the tension that had become a permanent part of his shoulders and neck these days. Along with the headache, bad attitude and piss-poor outlook on life. Unfortunately, the fact the review board had given him the promotion hadn't filled the hole inside him like he'd thought it would. Yes, it was more pay, more responsibility, and it gave him the ability to live anywhere in the Keys he liked, but it wasn't enough. It wasn't Lucy.

He leaned his elbow on the counter. "I guess."

"Problems with the leg laceration?" Luis arched a brow but didn't look up from the chart he was documenting in.

"Nope. Lucy did a good job fixing me up."

"Well, I'm glad someone finally did."

His brother's snark didn't improve Jackson's mood, but it wasn't Luis's fault the last place he wanted to be at that moment was work. Truthfully, he wanted to head straight back to Lucy's place and hold her until all the confusion and hurt and uncertainty inside him went away. Funny, but when he'd been with her, really with her, none of those demons had haunted him. When he was with her, all he felt was peace and serenity, completion, *worthiness*.

And that scared the bejesus out of him. "Uh, can we talk?"

Luis stared at him for a moment, then handed his chart to the nurse behind the desk before gesturing for Jackson to follow him down the hall to his office. "Have a seat."

He started toward the chairs in front of his

brother's desk, the limp barely noticeable anymore. His thigh was mostly healed, and the stitches had come out several days ago. Barely even ached at all. Jackson didn't allow himself to think about why that depressed him.

He started to sit when Luis gestured him away.

"Other one."

He barely stopped himself in time, then straightened and looked behind him, biting off a curse. A tiny creature blinked up at him. "Why's there a baby turtle in your office?"

His brother's tanned cheeks darkened a shade. Besides himself, the only other person he'd seen who could make his brother react like a schoolboy caught passing notes in study hall was Stacy Williams. They'd been spending a lot of time together lately, he'd noticed. Apparently, something big had happened between them during the storm, but Jackson hadn't quite worked it all out yet and he and his brother had both been too busy to sit down and discuss what they'd both been through like they needed to. Still, Jackson wouldn't usually miss a chance to razz his brother about it, but now he remained silent, feeling envious of his brother for the first time. It irritated the hell out of him.

"His owner's in the hospital, so I'm looking out for him until they recover," Luis said, pointing at the turtle. "Figured it might be good practice if we…"

The telltale signs of crickets chirping echoed through the office. Jackson would've noticed that right off if his mind hadn't been distracted…again.

He looked at Luis. "If we what?"

Luis shrugged and smiled slowly. "Stacy and I…"

Jackson still wasn't sure exactly what was going on, but based on the anticipation on his brother's face, it was something good. There was a time he'd feared Luis would let his work take over his life and never find the love he sought. Then Stacy had reappeared in his brother's life, and everything had changed. Sometimes joy came from the most unlikely of places.

That had certainly been true in Jackson's case, as Lucy's face filled his mind once more.

And he wondered—for the millionth time over the last two weeks—how she was doing, whether Mitzi's eggs had hatched, how the renovations were going. For his part, King was coping well with his amputation. The IV was gone and the kitten was moving around well, playing with his toys and eating his food, manipulating the hell out of Jackson for cuddles and treats at every opportunity. Now, if Jackson could just stop lying awake at night, aching for Lucy, they'd both sleep a lot better.

Luis sat back in his chair, staring at his brother with a narrowed gaze. "You haven't been the same since you came back from Big Pine Key. Something else happened during the hurricane."

It wasn't a question.

Jackson trusted Luis completely, and the feeling was mutual. His brother had never pushed him about what had happened during those twenty-four hours he and Lucy had been trapped together, same as Jackson hadn't pushed Luis about his history with Stacy. It was a code. An unspoken understanding. If they wanted to talk about it, they would. Eventually. But what Jackson really needed was advice on the rest of it. How to make a relationship work, how to even try to be that open, that vulnerable to someone, how to love a person when there was no guarantee they'd love you back or stay…

He stared at Luis for a long moment, then looked down at his toes. "Maybe."

"I thought so." Luis laughed. "So, what are you going to do about her?"

That was the question of the century. Part of him knew exactly what he wanted to do about Lucy. Jackson wanted to hug her and kiss her and apologize for making such a muck of things and beg her to take him back and let him try again. But the other part of him was still that scared little boy, watching his mother walk away from him forever and never wanting his heart ripped out like that again.

But in the end, his battered, scarred soul was done for anyway, when it came to Lucy.

Somehow, some way, she'd smashed through all his walls and claimed him the moment she'd asked for directions that day in the ER. Now, all he could think about was her cute smile and the cute way she counted things and the not-so-cute anxiety attacks she had when things got too overwhelming, and he wanted to be there for them all. Wanted to support her, in whatever way she needed him to, wanted to stand by her side and love her and grow old with her.

But she didn't need him, didn't want him there. Unless...

Jackson stared at his brother a moment, then turned to the baby turtle. It had worked once before. Did he dare hope it might work again? "You care if I take this little guy off your hands for a bit?"

"Why?"

"I think a vet should take a look at him."

Luis gave a lopsided smile then came around the desk to hand him the crate. "Take good care of him, brother. He belongs to my patient."

"Will do." Jackson peered inside the front

of the cage, walked to the door, then turned back. "My shift's over, so I might be gone for a few—"

"Take whatever you need. My patient won't be released until tomorrow, at least."

Jackson nodded. "Thanks, brother. I owe you one."

"Yes, you do." He chuckled, following Jackson out into the hall.

An hour and a half later, he thanked the captain of the boat he'd hired to take him from Key West and headed toward her compound on foot, the turtle cage in one hand and King under his other arm. He wasn't surprised to see things hadn't improved much in the two weeks since he'd left Lucy's compound on Big Pine Key. Mathilda had only brushed the coast before heading back out into the Gulf toward Texas, and most of the damage was outside the Keys. But Lucy had been lucky. Some of the smaller spits of coastal land had been flattened.

The first thing he noticed when he reached her place was that she'd moved most of the smaller bits of wreckage into rubbish piles near the perimeter of the compound, but most of the work still lay ahead. As he entered the grounds through a downed section of fence, he wondered if he'd be lucky enough to stay and help her with it. But luck had never been his claim to fame.

His grip tightened on the small crate he carried, and he looked down at King. "Well, guys, here goes nothing."

He was halfway to the house when he spied Lucy standing near the side of the pond, a pair of binoculars perched on her nose, Sam by her side.

His heart rate doubled, then tripled. Man, he was nervous. Maybe he was imagining all this. Imagining he'd found the one woman who made him feel whole, who knew him better than he knew himself, who saw his secrets and loved him, anyway. She whirled around when he was less than ten feet away, and he saw the reflection of the maelstrom inside him in her lovely dark eyes.

Nope. No imagining that.

"Jackson." As quickly as she'd said his

name, that mask of hers fell back into place again. But that one unguarded moment was all he needed. Her expression might be closed now, distanced, but he vowed one way or another, that wouldn't last long. Sam, of course, had no such reservations, rushing over to him, yipping and twirling around, demanding attention.

"What are you doing here?" Lucy asked, her gaze flickering to the squirming kitten under his arm. "Something wrong with King?"

"No." He set the turtle cage down then bent to scratch Sam behind the ears before straightening again and meeting her eyes.

Her gaze faltered for a split second, then held his firmly once more. "Oh. What then?"

Something heavy and hot in his heart shifted. "I needed to see you again."

"You did?" Her eyes widened slightly, then her shoulders squared, and her chin lifted. "Why?"

He pointed at the crate in his hand. "Luis and Stacy are caring for this little guy while the owner recovers, and they can't get him to eat. Thought maybe you could help." Then King meowed loudly, as if outraged to have been ignored so long. "And this little guy missed you and wanted to say hi."

"Oh."

Happy as Jackson would have been to watch his kitten running around the yard, playing with Sam like nothing had ever happened to him, the sheer disappointment in that one word from Lucy made him want to forget his plans and hug her tight right then, but he had to play this right. If he didn't, he could lose it all, and he wouldn't let that happen.

Not again.

Jackson wasn't certain of much at the moment, but the one thing he knew for sure was he wasn't going anywhere. Not now. Not yet. Maybe not ever, if he had his way.

"What's wrong with the turtle?" Lucy asked, shifting her attention to the small crate.

"Not sure. Maybe he needed to get out in the wild again."

"Then why bring him to me?" The hurt and uncertainty in her dark eyes was his undoing.

These two weeks apart had been torture, and Jackson was tired of dancing around the truth. "Because there is no one else, Lucy. There never will be. Not for me."

She stilled, looking at him, her expression...blank. Except for her gaze. Those deep, dark eyes.

Please let me in. Please believe in me.

Lucy turned her back then, and the hurt searing Jackson's chest nearly floored him.

Memories of his mother driving away for the last time flooded his mind, only to be quickly replaced by the joy he'd felt becoming a part of the Durand family. How he'd found new connections with them and Luis. How he wanted to start a new future with Lucy now. She wouldn't make this easy. Nothing about her was. That's why he loved her.

He stepped closer, keeping his hands at his sides, even though he wanted to touch her so much he ached. She'd lifted those damned binoculars of hers again and was staring across the pond, seemingly ignoring what he'd said.

After a few tense seconds, Jackson asked, "What are you looking at?"

"Mitzi's nestlings are hatching."

"They're okay?"

"Not sure if they'll all survive. Typically, they don't, but there aren't any natural predators around here, so their chances are dramatically improved."

"So the chances are—"

"Shh." She waved her hand to silence him. "Listen. Hear those tiny little gulping sounds?" Lucy turned to him, imitating the sound. "Like that."

His pulse pounded and his blood burned, but he kept his gaze on hers and strained his ears. "Yeah, I hear it."

"That's the nestlings. And if we can hear them from here, that means there's a bunch of them. Which means they made it, Jackson. They made it!"

He almost pulled her into his arms right then and there but stopped himself. *Patience, man.* He didn't want to give her any reason to run away from him again.

"Can we, uh, go to the clinic?" he asked,

his voice rough with need and emotion. "To talk?"

She nodded. After one last look across the pond, Lucy slipped her binoculars from around her neck, jotted some notes in the notebook she'd been carrying, then stuffed it all in the pocket of her baggy cargo shorts.

"I'm living in there for the time being," she said as they headed in that direction.

Once inside, he placed the turtle's crate on one of the long, shiny exam tables while she put away her stuff. King and Sam were playing with each other, chasing each other around in circles on the clinic floor. Jackson reached down to scratch King behind the ears when he hobbled over to him, then grinned at the kitten's loud purr.

"Looks like he's doing well," Lucy said, watching them. Jackson turned to find her across the room, leaning her hips against the edge of the sink, crossing her arms. "That's wonderful."

"Yeah. He's good."

Silence fell and his adrenaline spiked, igniting his blood. He swallowed hard. This was it. The big moment. But where to start?

The beginning. He needed to tell her everything. About his past. About why he'd acted the way he did that day at the helicopter.

"After my dad died in the war, life got hard, Lucy." The words emerged in a short burst, then he drew a long, shaky breath. "My mom had a hard time finding work because she had to take care of me, and we ended up on welfare. Eventually, we lost everything. Our house, our friends. We lived on the streets for a few months. She did the best she could, but I knew she wasn't happy. She cried a lot. I tried to help, but I was only four. Then one day, I guess she'd had enough. She got me dressed that morning, fed me my favorite cereal for breakfast, then walked me out to the car. I remember thinking it was weird that she'd packed my suitcase when we weren't going anywhere, but when I asked her about it, she wouldn't say why. Then we pulled up in front of a big brick building, and she got me out of the car. It was cold that day. So cold I could see my breath. She told me to sit on the steps and wait there until an adult came and got me. She told me to not forget my suitcase. She was crying."

His throat constricted and his eyes burned, but he kept going.

"She hugged me tight then. Tighter than she'd ever hugged me before. Then she got in the car and drove away. I watched those red taillights until I couldn't see them anymore, and then I started crying, too."

He sniffed and stared down at his toes.

"She left me. Abandoned me. I was so scared, but I still wanted to be with her. Even after all that, I thought if I was just better, she'd come back. If I just did enough, if I tried a little bit harder to be a good boy, to do the right thing. But she never did. Even after the Durands adopted me, and I got older, I never forgot her or what it felt like to not be enough. To not be worthy of love from the one person who should love you unconditionally. To be left behind by the one person who should never walk away. I used to dream of her at night sometimes as a kid, that she returned. That we had our old life back and we were a family again. But it didn't happen. I never heard a word from her again. She just disappeared from my life. I blamed myself."

"What...why?" Her voice shook with sadness. "Oh, Jackson. I'm so sorry."

"I was her son. I should have been enough, been there for her, but I couldn't." He scrubbed his hand over his short dark hair, gave an unpleasant laugh. "You were right. I think that's why I save people for a living. Make them all better. Because it made me feel worthy. Made me feel like I was something, like I mattered." He shook his head and dug the toe of his boot into the floor. "What hurts the most, though, is knowing she's out there somewhere, and that she wants nothing to do with me."

"Oh, Jackson."

He knew—*knew*—she understood, from the ache in her voice, the pain. But he had to get it out.

"So, yeah. I've spent my whole life trying to make myself worthy. By protecting those who needed my help, whether they wanted it or not. I joined the coast guard, became an EMT. Volunteered for the local Boys and

Girls Club. Whatever I can do to prove I am good enough, worthy enough for people to stick around and love. But it doesn't work. Because at the end of the day, I'm still the same old me."

"That's not true, Jackson. You are one of the best, most honorable men I know. You don't have to prove your worth. You're worthy of love just by being alive. And what she did was never your fault. Never," Lucy whispered, her tone edged with anguish. "You were only a child."

"Maybe." He shrugged. "I don't have any memories of my father, but I always thought he would want me to stand up for those who couldn't stand up for themselves." He looked up at her then. "And I did the best damn job I could. I gave it everything I had. But it didn't make a difference."

"Yes, it did, Jackson. It does make a difference. You're still helping people."

"But it's not enough. Because at the end of the day, I'm still alone. I thought by closing my heart, avoiding any kind of intimacy, I could keep from ever feeling that kind of anguish and abandonment again." He closed the distance between them and took her by the shoulders. "That I could avoid the pain of losing the people I loved. But it doesn't work. It never worked. The day I first came here, when I found King, I was on my way back from Miami. I mentioned it that day, but I didn't tell you why I'd gone up there. It was to get results from my DNA testing. I thought I'd try finding her one more time, maybe hire someone to track her down like they do on those TV shows or something. But then I met you, and suddenly it didn't seem to matter so much anymore. I finally feel like I'm ready to let that go, release the past and start fresh. With you. Do you understand, Lucy?"

"I think so." She nodded, her gaze guarded. "But you told me you don't want any messy ties. You want things to be neat. Fun. Clean. No complications." Her voice rose, shaking now. "So, where does that leave us?"

"I don't know." He lowered his head, putting his face close to hers. "Being with you during the storm changed me somehow. It's like there's this…emotional hole…inside me,

Lucy. And crazy as it sounds, I *know* you're the only one who can fill it."

She tried to pull free, but he held fast. "What happens when things get tough or someone else comes along? Someone easier, someone normal? You just walk away? You have another fling? Because I can't do that. I can't let you do that to me."

"I won't walk away, Lucy." He clenched his jaw so tight his ears popped. "I can't walk away, Lucy. Don't you see? I tried, these past two weeks, but I can't. I think about you constantly, worry about you. Want to be with you so badly it hurts. The hurricane made me realize that there are no guarantees in life, Lucy. The world isn't perfect. But locking myself in a box or a bubble thinking it made me safe only made me alone and miserable." When she didn't respond, a new doubt stabbed him in the chest. "Or don't you want me?"

Her eyes widened. "Yes, I want you! More than I've ever let myself want anything. When I turned around and saw you behind me out there, I knew I'd take whatever you had to give me, but…"

"But what?"

"I'm not sure I'll be enough for you."

"What?" Jackson said, clearly confused. "You're so brave and strong and confident. You are, Lucy."

Her resolve to stay distant crumpled in the face of his certainty, leaving her hollow and yearning inside. "If I let you in, give you my heart, and what you want turns out not to be me, it would kill me when you walked away, Jackson."

He cupped her face, his hold unbearably gentle. "Then I'll never do that, Lucy. I swear. Even when times get tough. Even when you tic like crazy and you count every step from here to Miami and back." She laughed, and he chuckled. "You are enough for me, Lucy. More than enough. The reason I said I didn't want anything more than sex was because I was terrified. Terrified of what you made me feel. Terrified because you filled that emptiness inside me. The one I'd tried for years to fill myself with meaningless flings and control and my need to protect others and avoid failure. But none of that worked. I kept you at a distance because I didn't let myself believe I could have you. Part of me still knows I don't deserve you. But when I looked into your eyes and saw myself, saw the other part of me, I knew."

Finally, he opened up and let his barriers all the way down, allowed her to see him, really see him—the vulnerability, the pain, the damage and flaws for the first time. "I knew you were the one for me. The only one for me. Lucy, I've never been so sure of anything in my entire life as I am of you."

His words scared her to death. They were complete opposites. And yet she loved him anyway, completely, unconditionally. The way she'd always wanted to *be* loved.

The longer she'd stayed at the compound alone, the more she realized everything had gone gray. Like she'd been cast into a barren wasteland. And the truth struck her like a death blow. Her knees buckled. Pinpoints of light flickered in the periphery of her vision, but Jackson was there, his warm, strong arms around her, holding her, supporting her, and she knew. Knew that if she didn't take this chance, with him, she'd regret it until the moment she drew her last breath.

Shoving her anxiety aside, she whispered hoarsely, "Jackson..."

He stared down at her, concern lining his handsome face. "What?"

"You really meant it, didn't you?"

"Of course. I've never lied to you."

Panic clawed at her throat, her need for control nearly overwhelming. So much rode on her response. Everything. Her whole life. Her future. A future with him. It could all be hers, if only she had the courage.

"I want you, too," she blurted, forcing the words out on a choked whisper. "More than I've ever wanted anything. But I'm scared."

"And you think I'm not?" He scowled.

"I don't know. You're braver than anyone I've ever known."

"You're brave, too, Lucy."

The way he said her name, like a prayer,

a benediction, made her heart slam against her rib cage.

"I thought Robert loved me, but he didn't. Not really. He just wanted to use me for research."

"I love you, Lucy." He held her tighter. "Real love. And screw Robert. If I ever meet him face-to-face, I'll punch him."

"I'd like to see that." She lowered her gaze. "But it's also about me not trusting myself. That's why I moved here. To prove to myself that I was strong and capable and not broken. That I could go it alone. But when I was with you during the storm, I realized those same needs to prove myself had crippled me, Jackson. They made me afraid to ever risk again. You were right about me, too. I thought if I never opened my heart to anyone again, if I stayed alone, I was guaranteed not to lose. I could have true freedom, but at what cost?"

"What are you telling me, Lucy?"

Now or never. She took that final step and met his gaze. "I'm telling you I'm sorry I hurt you. It's the very last thing I ever wanted to do. I'm sorry that I sent you away after the storm. I never meant to make you feel unworthy. You're the worthiest person I know."

Lucy pulled his face down to hers and kissed him hard. Put her heart, her life, her soul, everything she could say into it. He tensed, then accepted the fierce pressure of her mouth on his, but he didn't respond.

Dammit. She was losing him. Tears gathered in her eyes as she pulled away. "I'm sorry. I don't know what else to say. How else to apologize." Tears trickled down her cheeks. "Being scared was no excuse. I was wrong. I don't want you to go. I never wanted you to go."

It took a second, then his expression shifted to wariness. "What exactly are you saying?"

"I'm saying I love you, Jackson Durand. Don't leave. Don't walk away. And I swear I will never, ever, walk away, either."

"You'll never lose me, Lucy." This time he kissed her, hard. "Never."

"Thank God," she said, her sniffles turning to great gulping sobs. "I'm sorry... I can't seem...to stop..." She took a shuddering breath. "It's just I'm so—"

Jackson held her and tilted her face up to his. "I know, Lucy. I know."

She laughed and cried and hugged him again. "What a pair we are, huh?"

From his cage, Bubba squawked and danced across his perch, screeching, "Crazy in love."

"Lucy?" Jackson's voice was sweetly hoarse now.

"Mmm?" She nuzzled more deeply into his embrace, sighing happily when his arms tightened around her.

"Tell me again." He pressed his lips to her ear. "I need to hear you tell me again."

She smiled and gazed up at him once more. "I love you, Jackson Durand. For better, for worse. For always."

"I love you, too, Lucy Miller," he said, rubbing her arms. "It's scary, believing that I'm worthy of you, but I do. You make me believe it. And I promise to never let you down. I feel connected to you in a way I don't even understand yet. And I don't care. You're part of me, too. Always."

* * * * *